“I’m not in the habit of sleeping with a woman on such short acquaintance!”

Matt’s bluntness truly took the wind out of Clare’s sails.

“Of course,” he resumed, “I’m prepared to make an exception, under the circumstances.”

The breath zoomed back into her lungs—she was getting way out of her depth here. “And what do you mean by that?”

“I mean that if you’re desperate to go to bed, I’m rather tempted to oblige!”

MIRANDA LEE is Australian, living near Sydney. Born and raised in the bush, she was boarding-school educated and briefly pursued a classical music career before moving to Sydney and embracing the world of computers. Happily married, with three daughters, she began writing when family commitments kept her at home. She likes to create stories that are believable, modern, fast paced and sexy. Her interests include reading meaty sagas, doing word puzzles and going to the movies.

A VERY SECRET AFFAIR

MIRANDA LEE

MISTRESS MATERIAL

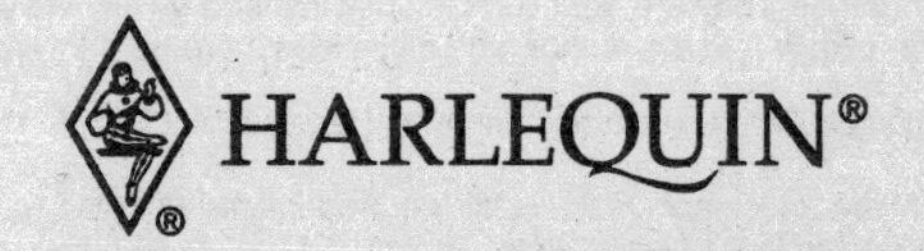

TORONTO • NEW YORK • LONDON
AMSTERDAM • PARIS • SYDNEY • HAMBURG
STOCKHOLM • ATHENS • TOKYO • MILAN • MADRID
PRAGUE • WARSAW • BUDAPEST • AUCKLAND

ISBN 0-373-80624-8

A VERY SECRET AFFAIR

First North American Publication 2002.

This edition published by arrangement with Harlequin Books S.A.

www.eHarlequin.com

Printed in U.S.A.

CHAPTER ONE

'AREN'T *you* the lucky girl!'

Clare put Mrs Brown's blood-pressure tablets plus the repeat of her prescription into the paper bag, then looked up with a frown on her face. 'What do you mean, lucky?'

Mrs Brown's expression was knowing and exasperated at the same time. 'Clare Pride! Who do you think you're kidding? I was just over at the town hall helping with the decorations for the deb ball tonight and I *saw* the names on the place cards on the main table. There's no use pretending you don't know what I'm talking about.'

Clare's heart fell. Oh, God. Surely her mother wouldn't have simply gone ahead and put her on that table against her wishes. Surely not!

'Fancy sitting next to the gorgeous Dr Adrian Archer all night.' Mrs Brown was almost swooning. 'That man can put his stethoscope on my chest any time he likes!'

For one mad moment Clare was in total agreement. She too had had her little fantasies while she watched *Bush Doctor* every Tuesday night without fail.

But she quickly remembered that that was all they were. Fantasies. The man on the screen was not real. He was an illusion. A romantic dream. In the flesh, he would no doubt prove to be the very opposite of the charming, caring, sensitive character he played on television.

One only had to read the women's magazines to get

the true picture. Hardly a week went by when his photograph didn't grace their pages, always with a different dolly-bird on his arm. Rumour had it he went through girlfriends like a hot knife through butter.

'He's not a *real* doctor, Nancy,' Clare pointed out drily.

Mrs Brown looked startled. 'Of course he's a real doctor! Look at all those emergency operations he's performed. Not only that, he has a simply wonderful bedside manner.'

I'll bet he has, Clare thought tartly.

'Only a real doctor could be as kind and warm and caring as Dr Archer is!' Mrs Brown pronounced firmly.

'Nancy,' Clare said patiently. 'He's an actor. No doubt there's a real doctor in the wings overseeing the authenticity of the scenes, but *Bush Doctor* is a television show with made-up towns and a made-up doctor. Dr Adrian Archer is *not* a real doctor. If you look at the credits at the end, you'll see he's played by an actor called Matt Sheffield.'

'Well he'll always be Dr Archer to me!' Mrs Brown sniffed, and, plonking down the exact coins for her prescription, swept up her parcel from the counter and marched from the shop.

Clare sighed her exasperation. Why couldn't women like Mrs Brown tell the difference between make-believe and reality? Why did they think characters in television serials were real people? And why, she thought wearily, do I have to be cursed with a mother who doesn't take no for an answer and who thinks she can run everything and everyone around her?

She glanced at her watch. It was almost twelve. In a few minutes old Mr Watson would take over—as he did every Saturday at noon—leaving her free for the afternoon. Usually she spent the time cleaning the flat upstairs and listening to music, but today a trip out home was called for.

There was no way Clare was even *going* to that ball tonight, let alone sit on the main table. She didn't want her enjoyment in her favourite television programme permanently spoiled. She wanted Dr Adrian Archer to *stay* Dr Adrian Archer. If she was forced to spend time with the real man behind the mask, how could she keep the fantasy man alive in her imagination? No, it was out of the question. Definitely out of the question!

It was all her mother's fault, of course. Really, she could not be allowed to get away with this. Give that woman an inch and she would take a mile!

Clare swung her dark blue Magna on to the deserted dirt road and put her foot down. The dust flew out behind her, spreading a red cloud over the still waters of the river alongside. She knew that speeding while angry was foolish, but she gave into it just this once, covering the distance from the turn-off to her parents' farm in half the usual time.

Samantha was walking her grey gelding, Casper, through the side gate when the Magna screeched to a halt in front of the rambling wooden house. 'Wow, sis!' she exclaimed as Clare scrambled out. 'You planning on entering a Grand Prix this year? What are you doing out here anyway? Shouldn't you be getting all dolled up for the big do tonight? You've only got seven hours left, you know. You'd better get started if you're to please Mum with the finished product.'

'Very funny, Sam. Where *is* Mum?'

'In her room, I think, making up her mind what to wear tonight. Brother, you sure look mad. What's she done now?'

'She's put me next to Matt Sheffield, that's what she's done!'

Sam launched herself into the saddle before frowning down at her sister. 'Who in heck's Matt Sheffield? I thought the guest of honor tonight was that doctor from *Bush Doctor*.'

'Matt Sheffield *is* the doctor from *Bush Doctor*.'

'So why are you complaining? Most of the old ducks in Bangaratta are ga-ga over him. Lord knows why. He's not that good-looking.'

Was the girl *blind*? The man was sensational-looking!

'And he's over thirty if he's a day,' Sam tossed off airily.

'Oh, over the hill, definitely.' Clare's tone was drily caustic. 'And thanks heaps, Sam. Am I classified as an old duck these days, am I?'

'Well, you are twenty-seven, sis. Twenty-seven and still single. Gosh, you're not even *living* with a guy. That might not make you an old duck, but it certainly makes you an old maid.'

'You don't live with a guy in Bangaratta, Sam. Not if you're the town pharmacist.'

'Then why come back, sis? Why didn't you stay in Sydney?'

Why indeed? Clare thought bitterly.

'You seemed happy there. This small-town life is not for you, you know.'

'So what's for me, Sam? Do tell me.'

Sam cocked her head on one side and gave her sister a brief but nonchalant once-over. 'Damned if I know, sis. But I know one thing. You shouldn't live anywhere near Mum. You two just don't get along. Gotta go. See you, sis.'

Samantha kicked the grey in the flanks and galloped off, her long blonde hair flying out behind her. Clare stared after her young sister, who looked older every time she saw her. She not only looked older but she was sounding older too.

Maybe Sam was right. Maybe she shouldn't have come home. But a fifteen-year-old teenager couldn't know what it was like to live in a big city, all alone with a broken heart.

Clare was walking towards the front steps, thinking bleak thoughts, when the front door was flung open by a tall, formidable-looking woman with short permed blonde hair, a big bosom and sharp grey eyes. Just my luck, Clare thought ruefully, to inherit the eyes and not the bosom.

'Oh, it's you, Clare. I thought I heard a car.'

Clare sighed. Occasionally she did crave to hear something like, Hello, darling daughter, how nice to see you, is there anything wrong and can I help you? As for a hug…she couldn't remember the last time her mother had hugged her. Hugging was not part of Agnes Pride's arsenal.

'What's up? You look frazzled. Perhaps you'd better come in for a cup of tea.'

Agnes was off down the hall before Clare could stop her. She followed her mother resignedly into the large, country-style kitchen at the back of the house, pulling out one of the high-backed wooden chairs that surrounded the kitchen table.

'Sam's growing up,' she remarked as she sat down.

'You know, I wouldn't be letting her go off on her own too much in future. Who knows who or what she might meet on the road, or in the bush?'

Agnes looked up from where she was filling the kettle with water, her mouth tightening. 'This is the country,' she said sharply, 'not your precious Sydney. Out here, girls are quite safe on their own. Besides, Samantha is fifteen and she's only going down the road half a mile to her friend's house. And it's not as though she's walking. She's riding a horse.'

'A horse is no match for a man, Mum. Not if he's got rape on his mind.'

'*Rape*? Girls don't get raped out here,' she scorned. 'We're a decent community, with decent morals.'

'Girls get raped everywhere, Mum,' Clare pointed out. 'Often by men they know.'

There was a short sharp silence as Agnes stared over at her daughter.

'Dear heaven,' she said at last. 'Is…is that what happened to you in Sydney, Clare? Is that why you came home so suddenly?'

'Good lord, no. No, nothing like that!'

'Then why *did* you come home out of the blue, then? You never did tell me.'

Clare opened her mouth then shut it again. She'd never felt comfortable confiding in her mother, who rarely gave constructive advice, only criticism. Agnes' staunchly old-fashioned morals had always precluded Clare's telling her the truth about her relationship with David. Her mother would have judged her harshly, then called her a fool. Clare craved sympathy and understanding, not condemnation. She knew only too well she'd been a fool!

'I just felt like coming home,' she hedged. 'I missed Bangaratta. Look, Mum, I haven't come out just to chat. I found out that someone has put me on the main table next to your guest-of-honour tonight and I013'

'*What*?' Agnes burst out. '*You've* been put next to Dr Archer?'

Clare realised immediately that she'd been wrong. It hadn't been her mother's doing at all!

'I'm going to give that Flora Whitbread a piece of my mind when I get there tonight,' Agnes blustered. 'I told her specifically that you didn't want to be on the main table. I even offered myself in your place. And what does she do? Puts you there anyway. Really, that woman's getting too big for her boots!'

Clare cringed at the thought of poor Flora getting an earful tonight. Frankly, if she'd known it was Flora's idea she might have gone along with it right from the start. She liked Flora. The old dear had a good heart and worked her socks off as president of the local progress committee. It had certainly been a feather in her cap to get someone like 'Dr Archer' as guest-of-honour for their local débutante ball. Flora was also hoping that the publicity might bring a real doctor to the small country town. Permanently.

Bangaratta's only doctor had retired last year due to ill health, and, while advertisements had been placed in newspapers all over the country, no one suitable had answered. Locals were having to travel to Dubbo for medical treatment, which was a highly unsatisfactory arrangement, especially for the elderly. Flora had vowed to move heaven and earth to rectify the situation.

'Flora probably wanted someone more Mr Sheffield's age to sit next to him,' Clare said by way of excuse. 'I guess she must have been desperate. All the other eligible young women in town are going to be debs. Don't say anything to her, Mum. I'll just sit there and suffer in silence.'

Agnes snorted. 'Suffer indeed! Most women would give their eye-teeth to be sitting where you will be tonight.'

Clare let that slide. Already she was feeling a little annoyed with herself for having backed down. The sacrifices one made for one's home town! Her Tuesday nights would never be the same again.

Agnes finished making the tea, carrying a tray over to the table. No teabags for Agnes Pride. Two cups were poured, the milk added then one cup and saucer put precisely in front of Clare, the other carried down to the opposite end of the oval table. Agnes sat down, her back straight as she lifted the cup to her lips, her sharp eyes flicking over her first-born as she sipped the hot liquid.

Clare fell silent while she drank down the hot tea in long, painful swallows. Why did her mother always have to look at her like that? As if she was attempting some sort of mental make-over, yet all the time believing a satisfactory result was impossible.

'You really should get your hair cut, Clare,' Agnes said. 'Down, it looks straggly and unkempt. And that bun you wear for work makes you look like a spinster. A little make-up wouldn't go astray either. You have a very nice complexion and your eyes are quite lovely, but there's always room for improvement. Not only that, how do you expect to catch a man's eye wearing trousers all the time? Men like to see a woman's figure.'

'My first priority in life is not to catch a man's eye, Mum. And I don't wear *trousers*. I wear jeans. A man can see as much of a woman's figure in jeans and a T-shirt as a dress. Sometimes more.'

'So we're to look forward to your showing up at the ball in jeans tonight, are we?' came the tart remark. 'I'm sure Dr Archer will be impressed.'

'Matt Sheffield is his name, Mum. Dr Archer is the character he plays on television.'

Agnes' blank blink showed she was as much a victim of the illusion as Mrs Brown.

'I do happen to own a ballgown or two,' Clare continued. 'I have one that is especially nice. Still, I doubt anything *I* could wear or do would genuinely impress a man of Mr Sheffield's ilk.'

'Don't be ridiculous, Clare. You can be quite attractive when you want to be.' Agnes plonked her cup noisily into the saucer. 'Tell me! *Why* do you dislike Mr Sheffield so much? Have you met him before, is that it? I know you used to go to the theatre a lot when you lived in Sydney.'

Clare put down her cup also, rattling it slightly. 'No, I've never met him. But handsome male actors are all tarred with the same brush. They think they're God's gift to women, when in fact they're from the devil.'

An image filled her mind, of a curtain going up and a man stepping on the stage, a rivetingly handsome man. He'd looked like a Greek god. But there'd been nothing heavenly about David in the end. He'd consigned her to hell and left her there.

'You've become very cynical, Clare. Sometimes I wish you'd hadn't gone away to Sydney.'

'You and me both,' Clare muttered, a curl of pain squeezing her heart.

'No one forced you.' Her mother sounded indignant. 'You were all for going.'

All for getting away from you, you mean, Clare thought, then felt guilty. Despite their differences, she did love her mother. But Sam was right. They didn't always get along. 'I didn't have much choice, you know, Mum,' she soothed. 'Bangaratta is hardly the education capital of the world.' She stood up and carried her cup and saucer over to the sink. 'I'd better be going. I guess I'll be seeing you tonight after all.'

Agnes walked with her to the door.

'What's this dress like that you're going to wear?' she asked once they reached the front veranda. 'Are you sure it isn't out of fashion? You have been back here in Bangaratta a couple of years, after all.'

'It'll do, Mum,' Clare said, aware that this was a wicked understatement of the truth.

Agnes sighed. 'I suppose it'll have to, but it's a pity for our guest to think that the ladies of Bangaratta don't know how to dress. Country does not mean dowdy!'

Something deep and dark darted through Clare. 'Some people think so,' she murmured, but at her mother's quick frown, Clare forced a bright, if somewhat brittle smile to her lips. 'I doubt Mr Sheffield will give a hoot what I wear, Mum, but don't worry, I won't let you—or Bangaratta—down.'

The Bangaratta Town Hall hadn't looked this grand in years, Clare thought. Built in 1886, it had always been the focal point of the small bush town. This was where the dances were held, the meetings, the wedding receptions. It had even doubled as the schoolhouse till the 1920s when the success of the wheat crops brought an upsurge in population and, of course, more schoolchildren. Of late, the building had been looking shabby, but tonight...tonight there was fresh paint on the walls, the windows sparkled, the wooden floor gleamed and high above, banners, balloons and streamers lent a festive spirit.

Clare walked up on to the wooden stage where the main table was located, her eyes sliding from her name card to the splendid table setting. Who would have believed that underneath the crisp white tablecloths and bowls of fresh flowers lay plain wooden trestles?

Flora and her progress committee had outdone themselves this time. Why, even the cutlery was not the usual catering stuff, but genuine silver. Clare gazed down at the spruced-up old building with a sense of pride. Not the sort of sophisticated venue Matt Sheffield was probably used to, she conceded, but still, it looked its very best. As did she...

Clare's heart contracted. There was a certain irony in wearing this particular dress tonight which did not escape her. The dress had remained in her wardrobe, unworn, as a symbol of her hurt and a warning never to be so stupid again.

She was only wearing it tonight because she'd been goaded into it by her mother—she had another dress which would have sufficed—but she supposed it was a good thing in a way. It was time to exorcise the ghosts once and for all. Time to show the world—and Bangaratta—that she was not old maid material after all.

The thought of the expression of her mother's face when she saw her designer-clad daughter *did* give Clare some satisfaction. Not only was her dress an original worth many hundreds of dollars, but the rest of her matched it for style and sophistication. Her hair, despite being out, was definitely not straggly. She'd spent all afternoon putting a warm red rinse through its mid-brown colour, then shampooing, setting and styling it till it bounced around on her shoulders in a profusion of large loose curls, coppery highlights dancing on the crests of the waves that curved sleekly around her face.

Aah, yes…her face. Normally left *au naturel*, that too had received a lot of attention. She had spent a long, agonising hour painstakingly applying the sort of make-up that made the most of even the plainest girl. A bronze gloss now shimmered on her expertly outlined lips; blusher emphasised her good cheekbones; and after a careful application of misty eyeshadows, eyeliner and mascara, her grey eyes had taken on a more mysterious look, as opposed to the cool clarity she usually presented to her customers across the counter of the shop.

Of course, it was the dress, in the main, that would draw eyes, a turquoise Thai silk gown with a wide off-the-shoulder wraparound collar, a fitted waist and a gathered skirt which curved up and down at the front to show her best asset—her long athletic legs. With a push-up strapless bra underneath, she had contrived enough cleavage to be interesting, knowing that a lot of men were tantalised more by what was hinted at than what was flaunted.

Not for the first time that evening, Clare wondered if Matt Sheffield would find her attractive. Her innate honesty forced her to concede she hadn't gone to all this trouble just for her mother.

Clare was a woman, after all. What woman wouldn't want to look her best in the presence of a man as handsome and sophisticated as Matt Sheffield? Pride demanded it. Or was it something else which had prompted her to pull out all the stops?

Clare's heart began to race nervously as she stared at the place she would fill at the table on the stage. Within half an hour she would be sitting there, next to the sort of man whose *real* character she knew oh so well. And while Clare knew she wasn't a raving beauty, she was far from plain. Her mother would have been astounded at the number of men who had tried to chat her up since her return home.

Yes, she was not so unattractive that their visitor wouldn't take a second look. What worried her was how she would act if he started flirting with her, or even made a pass? She hoped her foolish female heart would be able to differentiate the actor from the doctor he played on television. There was no doubt Mrs Brown was right about one thing. Dr Adrian Archer did have a marvellous bedside manner!

Clare dragged in then expelled a shuddering sigh. She should not have agreed to this. No matter what. She had very bad vibes about it.

'Clare! Yoo-hoo, Clare!'

Clare looked down into the body of the hall to see Flora waving at her from near the back doors. With a resigned sigh she made her way over, trying not to cringe over the dress Flora was wearing—a loud floral which looked hideous on her plump figure. The poor sweet darling was also all pink and flustered as she kept checking arrivals out the back.

'Oh, my, don't you look simply stunning!' Flora praised between anxious peers. 'I…er…hope you didn't mind about my putting you on the main table after all, dear. I was speaking to your father in town this morning and he said you must have misunderstood what I wanted because he was sure you wouldn't mind at all. I…er…hope he was right.'

Clare smiled. 'He was perfectly right. I just thought maybe you could find someone better suited than me, that's all.'

'Oh, goodness me, no. I told Jim that there wasn't a brighter or prettier girl in town than you and if anyone could charm our guest it would be our own darling lady chemist.' Flora suddenly squealed and grabbed Clare's wrist. 'Oh, look. There's his car! Isn't this thrilling?'

Clare pulled out of the other woman's grasp, alarmed to find that her heart was galloping. She also found herself joining Flora in the avid peering through the doorway.

A shiny black car was rolling into the kerb. When it stopped, a man in a black dinner suit slid out from behind the wheel. A tall man. A nice-looking man. He wasn't, Clare recognised with sick relief, the man himself.

'That would be Mr Marshall. He's our guest's manager. Oh, there's Dr Archer, getting out now. Aren't you coming down to meet him?'

Clare swallowed, finding her eyes riveted on the opening passenger door. 'No,' she croaked.

'Well, I certainly am.' Flora surged down the steps towards the welcoming committee.

The passenger door was wide open now and a sleek dark head appeared, connected to a black dinner suit. Clare did not wait to see any more. Totally unnerved, she turned and fled back into the hall.

CHAPTER TWO

CLARE shut the door of the back-stage powder-room and leant heavily against it. Literally shaking, she tried to calm her thumping heart and failed miserably.

Finally she managed to still the ragged, painful breathing that her mad flight had caused. Levering herself away from the door, she walked over to the seat that ran along one wall of the small rest-room.

Thank the lord, she thought as she sank down, that no one had seen her hurtling down the hall and stumbling up the stage steps. She would be eternally grateful for a country town's obsession with the rich and famous, grateful that all eyes had been fixed elsewhere.

Clare closed her eyes and leant back against the wall. Just a few minutes, she told herself. A few minutes so that she would feel collected enough to return to the hall and take her place at the main table.

What on earth had caused her to panic like that? So she found the man attractive? So what? She had found any number of men attractive over the years. She'd even been attracted to a couple of local men since coming home. Unbeknown to her mother, she'd gone out with them too, thinking that in Bangaratta she might find a man of principle she could fall in love with and possibly marry.

But in truth, Clare had found the local men so boring, their personalities so flat and dull, that she now lived a lonely life rather than keep seeking an elusive dream.

Clare stood up and walked slowly towards the mirror that hung above the washbasins. Her eyes travelled slowly over her hair, her dolled-up face, her glamorous gown. When she went to push back a stray hair she was dismayed to see her hands were trembling. With a groan she leant against the bench and stared into the basin. When she glanced up again she was hotly aware of the over-bright eyes, the still racing heart.

Face it, she warned herself in a harsh whisper. The man excites you. The man himself...*not* the character on television. Why else have you avidly read everything printed about him? Those articles were about Matt Sheffield, *not* Dr Adrian Archer.

That's why you refused to come tonight in the first place: because, underneath, you knew he was too much like David for your peace of mind. Both exceptionally handsome men. Both brilliant actors. Both, amazingly, the only sons in wealthy Sydney families, each even more amazingly headed by a politician patriarch. The similarities were quite striking.

OK, so David had given up acting shortly after leaving university to pursue a career in a law firm, presumably with his eye on politics. But lawyers and politicians were consummate actors anyway, Clare reasoned cynically.

Given his similar background, it was hard to see Matt Sheffield turning out any differently from the smoothly polished, superbly arrogant and insidiously charming type David had been. But beneath the surface appeal would lie a soul so shallow and insincere, so utterly, utterly selfish, that such a man should wear a brand across his forehead declaring to the world at large—and women in particular—that they were poison.

Oh, yes, Clare knew exactly what to expect tonight. Yet even so, the prospect of being in Matt Sheffield's company had stirred her as no man had since David.

Fortunately, being forewarned was forearmed. With her past bitter experience to the forefront of her mind, Clare felt reasonably confident she could sustain a coolly polite façade all night, no matter how attractive she found the man, or how much he flirted with her. Any direct defensive rudeness was out of the question, of course. Flora and Bangaratta were counting on her.

Steeling herself, Clare left the rest-room. She had just walked past the gents' room and her foot was on the first of the three steps that led back up into the right wing of the stage when a man's exasperated voice pulled her up short. 'Good God, Bill, this place is a lot more back-woods than I expected.'

'You're not wrong there. Did you get a load of the decorations? Bloody balloons, no less! Why on earth you accepted this invite, I have no idea. The appearance fee won't even cover expenses. As for publicity…you don't need that any more.'

'Certainly not of the nature I've been getting. But I agree, this doesn't seem to have been one of my better decisions. Talk about the back of Bourke!'

Clare cringed inside. She knew instinctively whom that superbly cultured voice belonged to. She'd heard it often enough on the TV. Normally, she liked its deep rich tones, especially when it was soothing an accident victim, or a woman in painful childbirth. But overhearing it utter words flavoured with sarcasm and contempt reminded her of that other highly educated voice from the past, brutally putting her down because she was country born and bred. The memory brought a rush of rage that overpowered her resolve to remain cool and she hurried forward to confront this pair who dared speak disparagingly of her home town.

The two men were standing between the two sets of heavy stage curtains, their backs towards her, but their broad-shouldered, dauntingly male figures made Clare hesitate. When they resumed speaking, she found herself retreating behind a backdrop.

'I'm certainly not looking forward to a whole evening of that woman's inane chatter,' Matt Sheffield said wearily.

'You mean Mrs Pride?'

'No, the other one. In the revolting floral dress. Flora something or other. But they both descended on me like a plague of locusts. Thank God you came to the rescue. I wouldn't have thought to suggest a trip to the gents.'

'That's what I'm paid to do. Not that you really needed rescuing. You always handle women very well.'

Matt Sheffield's laughter was dry. 'Only some, Bill, only some. I suppose you heard I've been partnered with Miss Clare Pride for the evening, daughter no doubt of the aforementioned Mrs Pride. God, what a ghastly woman!'

'Come now, Matt, Mrs Pride wasn't too bad. Try to look on the bright side. Perhaps Miss Pride will be as well endowed as her mother.'

Clare blushed all over. Whether from anger or a sharp feeling of inadequacy, she didn't know. She was too enraged to think clearly!

'The way my luck is going lately,' the guest-of-honour continued, 'she'll be a flat-chested spinster whose only vice is butterfly collecting.'

Their mutual laughter sealed their fate. Or it did in

Clare's eyes. Just you wait, Mr Sheffield, she plagiarised. Just you wait...

Clare stayed where she was hidden for a couple of minutes, and when she emerged her smiling face hid an iron-willed determination to see that man in hell.

The guest-of-honour was by now standing behind his chair at the main table, with the man called Bill two chairs down on his left, Flora between them. Clare thought she was mentally prepared to meet her foe, but as she crossed the stage he swung round and fixed the most incredible blue eyes on her. She found herself speechless and staring, almost as hard as she was being stared at. With one shattered glance she took in the splendid cut of his tall figure, the well-shaped mouth, the manly chin with its tiny cleft, the strong nose, the sweep of dark brown hair. But always, in the centre of her stunned appraisal, those gorgeous blue eyes.

She must have shaken his hand, said something in greeting. She couldn't remember. It was just as well she noticed the raised-eyebrow glance he flicked Bill's way and the slight smugness that crossed the other man's face. So, the exchange seemed to say. This is a turn-up for the books. Not so bad after all.

At least that was what Clare imagined they were thinking, and it was enough to snap her out of her fatuous reaction to the man.

God! How could I? she castigated herself inwardly. So the man has incredible eyes. You already knew that, you idiot!

Unbeknown to her, a look of sheer disgust slid into her own expressive grey eyes, freezing Matt Sheffield on the spot. He frowned, but was immediately distracted by Clare's parents joining them.

'Matt, did you meet Jim Pride?' Flora gushed. 'He's Agnes' husband and father of our lovely Clare here. Jim is our local bank manager. Fancies himself a farmer on the weekend, though.'

Everyone laughed. Everyone, that was, except Clare, who was still shaken by her own treason. How *could* she let herself gawk at the man like an adolescent schoolgirl? It was enough to have admitted earlier she might find his company stimulating, but to be going weak at the knees…

'Yes we have met, Flora,' her father said, while flashing an appreciative glance his daughter's way. 'We're very proud of Clare, aren't we, Mother?' This while linking arms with a startled Agnes. 'She's a pharmacist, you know. Worked in Sydney for a while, but decided to come home a couple of years ago.'

Matt Sheffield's mouth smiled at her again, but not the eyes. This surprised Clare. Most womanisers used their eyes to advantage all the time. Had he sensed her ambivalence perhaps? Did it bother him that she had not continued to devour him visually as most women would have? She hoped so.

'I dare say,' he drawled, 'that the local lads are grateful for that.'

More laughter and an angry colour from Clare. Of course, she reasoned bitterly, a woman is never to be congratulated for her academic achievements, just reminded of her prime function in life: that of being a sex object, a mere decoration, placed here on earth for the sole purpose of pleasuring the male of the species.

'You're embarrassing our girl,' Flora admonished, but coyly. 'Besides, she doesn't always look as glamorous as this, do you, Clare? Your visit has brought out the best in Bangaratta.'

Clare found this supposedly soothing remark even more humiliating, as though she had deliberately gone out and tarted herself up, just for *this* man's benefit—a fact that was disturbingly close to the truth. She saw the speculation in that blue-eyed gaze and felt like cutting Flora's tongue out, the soft-hearted fool!

'Everyone and everything looks marvellous,' the guest-of-honour flattered, his gaze sweeping the hall.

Oooh! You hypocrite, she fumed, but kept her mouth clamped firmly shut. He would keep.

'We've done our best,' Agnes said with pompous pride.

Clare was happy to fall silent and let her mother and Flora hold the stage. Empty chit-chat continued and it was only the appearance of several ladies anxious to serve the banquet dinner which was to precede the presentation of the débutantes that made everyone finally sit down.

Clare was relieved to find Stan Charters seated on her right. He was the local grocer, a fat jolly man in his fifties, another member of the local progress committee and quite a talker.

'You're looking particularly delightful tonight, Clare,' Stan complimented her warmly straight away. 'That's some dress!'

'Why, thank you, Mr Charters,' she said sweetly. With a bit of luck she'd be able to chat away to him all night and totally ignore Matt Sheffield. In approximately four hours, she continually reassured herself, she would be safely back in her flat, and this little episode would be nothing more than a bad memory.

But Mr Charters was not to be Clare's saviour. Her mother was seated on his other side and constantly claimed his undivided attention. Flora, who was seated between Mr Sheffield and Mr Marshall, was a valuable ally for a while, buttering up her prized guest with a stream of compliments. Bearing witness to such effusive flattery had a detrimental effect on Clare's already nettled frame of mind, however, so that when Flora turned her attention to Mr Marshall on her left, and Matt Sheffield did turn to speak to her, she was hard pushed to be civil.

'Those were very good prawns,' he said to her as she was about to dissect the last one in her seafood cocktail. The note of surprise in his smooth voice did nothing to help her antagonism.

'They're Sydney prawns,' she informed him. 'Probably flown in especially for you.'

'Aah... Nothing better than a good Sydney prawn.'

'I dare say.' Her tone was bored. She could feel his eyes on her but be damned if she was going to give him the satisfaction of turning in his direction.

'And why, Miss Pride,' he asked softly after a few seconds' silence, 'would you want to bury your considerable talents in a small country town?'

She took a steadying breath, dampening down the upsurge of irritation. This time she did turn her eyes his way, deceptively wide and innocent eyes. '*Bury*, Mr Sheffield? This is my home, not a cemetery. I like living here. But aside from that, I was also needed here. Bangaratta's only chemist was getting too old to work full time and they couldn't get anyone else. We're having similar trouble filling the position of town doctor after our last physician had to retire through ill health.

Professional people these days seem reluctant to go bush.'

He was nodding. 'So Flora told me. She also explained the sort of commitment a doctor would have to make if he came to work here. The money might be good but the workload and hours are horrendous. Not too many doctors are prepared to make such a commitment.'

'Commitment does seem to be a problem with men these days,' she said, trying not to sound sour.

'Not all doctors are men,' he pointed out. 'Maybe a woman doctor would be better suited. Or were you thinking of killing two birds with the one stone?'

'In what way?'

He smiled in what seemed like a secret amusement. 'Why, supplying the town with a doctor and yourself with a suitable life-partner, of course. I would imagine a highly intelligent and attractive lady like yourself might be hard to satisfy in that regard. Tell me, Miss Pride,' he said, teasing lights glittering in his beautiful blue eyes, 'do you personally interview all the applicants? Is that why the right man hasn't been found for the job yet?'

Clare could have reacted to this provocative sparring in a few different ways. She could have blushed prettily—except she hadn't blushed like that in years and didn't think she could rustle one up. She could have come back with a suitable put-down. Hell, she should be good at those. Living with her mother had given her plenty of practice at sarcasm. Or she could try a hand at the sort of witty repartee she hadn't indulged in for three years. There hadn't been anyone in her life lately who liked that kind of thing.

Clare knew that to do so went against the way she had vowed to act tonight, but she couldn't seem to stop herself.

'Well actually, Matt,' she murmured, leaning his way in a highly flirtatious fashion, 'there was this one divine-looking chap last week who had potential, but I took him to dinner then back to my flat for a more in-depth interview, and quite frankly, he just didn't measure up.' With this, she dropped her eyes down to his crotch, then back up to his face. 'It's a pity that you're not a real doctor, because I'm sure I'd give an application from you one hell of a thorough looking into.'

His delighted chuckle did things to her nerve-endings that should have been warning enough. But, like all forms of intoxication, such dizzying effects were easy to become addicted to. Clare had forgotten what it was like to be in the company of an attractive sexy, clever man, and to have him dance attention on her. Quite suddenly, she was loving it.

'This evening is turning out to be far more entertaining than I ever imagined,' he said smilingly, his eyes caressing hers. 'So tell me, Clare, how long did you live in Sydney?'

She noted his dropping of the Miss Pride tag, but could find no fault in it. She liked the sound of her name on his tongue, liked the way Matt had rolled off hers.

'Seven years.'

'Seven years! You must have gone into withdrawal when you came back here. Don't you miss the bright lights, the faster pace of living?'

Yes, she did miss those things, had never stopped missing them. Sometimes she simply longed for a night out at the theatre or the ballet. Or just a stimulating evening's chat with the circle of friends she'd once had. No…be strictly honest, a tiny voice said. They were David's friends. Never yours.

'I…I like Bangaratta,' she defended, but not with much conviction.

'You surprise me. You look…out of place here.' He picked up his wine glass and as he sipped, his eyes continued to hold hers. God, they were beautiful, those eyes, and far, far too intuitive.

'What looks out of place,' she said, glancing away as she pushed her plate away, 'is the dress.'

Her breaking eye-contact plus the memories the dress brought back snapped Clare out of her momentary weakness. God, what did she think she was playing at here? Where was her damned pride? Get this conversation back on track before you make a right fool of yourself.

'So, will *Bush Doctor* continue into the New Year?' she asked abruptly. 'I only ask because the women around here would die if the wonderful Dr Adrian Archer wasn't there to fill their empty Tuesday evenings.' She hadn't meant to sound sarcastic, merely matter-of-fact, but somehow a caustic tone had crept in.

'I see you're not a fan yourself,' he returned slowly.

'I watch it occasionally,' she lied.

'But you can live without the wonderful Dr Adrian Archer.'

His drily mocking tone got to her. 'I certainly can. I can live without the man *behind* the mask too.'

He was stunned, she could see, jerking back in his seat to stare at her. For her part, she was instantly consumed with shame and guilt.

'I'm sorry,' she blurted out. 'That was unforgivably rude of me. Please…I…I don't know what got into me.

You've been so kind, coming all this way, and now I've spoiled things.' Tears of frustration were distressingly close.

His hand unexpectedly closed over hers where it lay clenched on the table and when she looked up she noticed for the first time the dark shadows around his eyes, the weary lines of exhaustion. My God! The man's tired, she realised. Terribly, terribly tired.

'It's all right, Clare,' he murmured. 'Obviously I must have said or done something to upset you. Perhaps you thought I overstepped the mark earlier, that I was coming on to you. If that's the case, then I'm sorry.' He looked deeply into her eyes, holding her. 'Really sorry...'

For a few breathtaking moments she was almost taken in.

Wait on there, experience jumped in to warn her. Maybe he is tired, maybe his defences are genuinely down, maybe his irritation backstage was just exhaustion talking and not contempt. But only maybe. I'm the lost sheep here, remember? The only one around not worshipping at his altar. Tread carefully.

'I think we should get on with our dinner, don't you, Mr Sheffield?' she said stiffly.

He nodded and Clare sighed inwardly with relief. God, she'd almost made two *faux pas* then. Not only insulted the man but almost been won over by him. Not that she could entirely blame herself. He was even more devastatingly attractive than David. He exuded sex appeal and threw charming lines as cleverly as a fisherman. Plenty of women would be caught by such a bait, but not sensible once-bitten Clare.

As if to prove her wrong, they had just finished the main course when he leant close. 'I have a favour to ask of you.' His breath was warm against her cheek. It stirred her hair and much, much more.

'When the dinner and débutante business is over,' he continued in that same low, husky tone, 'don't leave me in the clutches of Flora Whitbread. Stick by my side. Promise?'

She nodded, all coherent thought and resolve gone out the window. She hardly noticed the lady taking her empty plate and replacing it with dessert.

'And do call me Matt,' he added quietly.

Matt...

A smooth name for a very smooth man. God but she was weak. How could she possibly be letting herself be taken in by him?

'Something wrong, Clare?'

She looked up to find Matt frowning over at her. 'You haven't touched your dessert,' he pointed out.

Her grey eyes narrowed, seeing not his face sitting beside her, but another equally handsome face. The memory was sharp, the pain momentarily strong. And then her gaze cleared. 'Sorry,' she muttered. 'I was away in another world.'

Matt was still frowning at her. 'Not a happy one,' he commented. 'Is there anything I can do?'

'No,' she said far too sharply. You'd be the last man on earth who could wipe away my pain, Matt Sheffield! She picked up her dessert fork and jabbed at the cheese-cake.

Over coffee, Flora stood up and made a blessedly short but simpering speech of gratitude to their guest-of-honour. Matt's reply was a witty, obviously off-the-cuff speech which mentioned Bangaratta's plight in not having a town doctor. A few journalists were there, taking notes, Clare saw, and the photographers were busily snapping away. Who knew? Maybe some good would come of this. When Matt sat down, the applause was deafening.

'You were marvellous,' she said when he looked across at her. And she meant it. She wasn't so prejudiced that she couldn't give praise when praise was due.

His stare was so intense that Clare imagined he was in fact reading her mind. 'True praise indeed,' he said in a low voice, 'when it comes from a hostile audience.'

She scooped in a sharp breath. 'Matt, I…'

'Come now, Clare.' His smile was sardonic. 'This man behind the mask is not a sensitive creature.' He fixed a deadly eye on her. 'You have it in for me for some reason, but be damned if I know what it is.'

Her face must have confirmed his guess.

'What? No further apologies?'

For a moment she thought of Flora's committee and distress flashed into her eyes.

'Don't back down. I like honesty. But I must admit I have found your attitude quite intriguing. What have I done, I ask myself, to instil such antagonism in the most desirable woman I have ever met?'

It was a suitably tantalising note to end their conversation on. And he knew it, Clare decided, watching agitatedly as he joined Flora and Co. for the presentation of the débutantes. Clare could only stare after him, her stomach in knots. With that parting shot he had stirred up a hornet's nest inside her. Oh, Matt, you are a clever, clever man, she realised through her fluster.

'Clare…'

Clare's head jerked round at her mother's voice.

'Something wrong, dear?' came the enquiry. 'You look…flushed.'

Clare drummed up a covering smile. 'I'm all right. A slight headache. I might go home soon.'

'But you can't do that! The debs are about to be presented. And you might be needed later to help entertain the guest-of-honour. Come over and sit down with me and your father.'

Clare sighed and gave in graciously. It was the best way with her mother.

The music started up—it was taped music, the committee unable to afford an orchestra or a band on top of their expensive guest. Clare sat in silence while the five white-gowned girls were presented, listening while her mother raved on about how lovely they looked, how charming their guest was and how wonderful the night had turned out to be. She determined to slip away once the official proceedings were over and the dancing began. Someone else could help 'entertain' the guest-of-honour.

It didn't prove to be that easy. People kept claiming her attention, all of them eager to tell her how stunning she looked. Still, after her mother's disappointing silence on the subject, it was some balm to her ego and she couldn't say she disliked the flattery. Not only that—while she was busy chatting to the townsfolk, she was safe from the enemy's attentions.

Not that she wasn't aware of where he was and what he was doing every single moment. One only had to find the largest circle of women and there he would be, holding court in the middle of them. Truly, the man was a menace. He was standing at that moment with a group of elderly women who were all laughing and smiling.

Clare felt a reluctantly admiring smile pull at her mouth as she watched him in action.

Suddenly he turned his head and caught her eye. For a moment he just stared and then he turned aside and whispered something to Bill Marshall. Clare knew instinctively that this interchange had something to do with her, and a wave of unease swept through her. She watched, with increasing alarm, as Bill made his way towards her.

'Care to dance, Clare?'

She blinked her surprise but quickly found herself on the dance floor.

'Matt said to tell you he'd be leaving shortly, ostensibly to go back to the motel. But he wants to know if he could meet you somewhere private for a drink.'

Clare was dumbfounded. And furious! She'd heard of pop stars sending their henchmen out to collect some groupies for the night, but this...this was outrageous!

'Tell me, Bill,' she began with an innocent air, 'do you always procure Matt's women for him? Or is it only on these out-of-town jaunts?'

Bill didn't appear the slightest bit offended. Clearly being unflappable and unoffendable were required qualities in a big-time agent. 'I see,' came the cool reply. 'I presume the answer, then, is no.'

'Please don't presume, Bill,' she swept on, her voice cool but her heart pounding with anger. 'I wouldn't dream of turning down such a prize. I just hope he realises that a drink will be all he'll be getting!'

'Matt is a gentleman,' he stated, then added with what Clare thought considerable irony, 'Where can he meet you?'

Clare could hardly believe this was happening. Two

years of dealing with country men had made her forget how daring and aggressive some city men could be. They did what others only thought about. Her temper rose, her vow earlier in the night to see this man in hell catapulting back into her brain. She couldn't deliver hell exactly, but she sure as heck would teach him a lesson or two!

'I live in a flat above the pharmacy in the main street,' she said, smiling. 'There's access from the back lane. I'll leave the porch light on. Tell him to just walk up the steps and knock.'

'You leave first,' Bill said, projecting a secrecy Clare found disgusting, though predictable. 'Matt will be with you as soon as he can.' He strode briskly away, a hint of smugness playing on his lips.

She stared after him, still disbelieving. She watched him go up to Matt, held her breath as he whispered in his ear. Matt was frowning and then his head was turning. Those incredible blue eyes locked with hers. Her heart stopped, then seemed to tremble.

My God, what had she just done?

For the second time that night, Clare fled.

CHAPTER THREE

CLARE paced nervously around her flat. Every now and then she would stop and rearrange the pillows on her oversized sofa, unaware that such an action might have Freudian overtones. She kept going to the back window and looking out into the lane, one moment hoping that he would hurry and the next wishing he'd never turn up.

She spun away from the window for the umpteenth time and resumed her pacing. God, what a fool I am! A blithering idiot to think I can play at games like this. The man's dangerous. Here I am, hating him for his arrogance, his presumption, plotting to take him down a peg or two, yet, underneath, trembling with anticipation and excitement.

A sharp rap on her door sent her into a spin.

He'd come...

With her heart hammering inside her lungs she fairly raced to the door. Just in time did she pull herself up, steady her breathing, drum up a mechanical smile. She opened the door. 'Did you have any trouble finding the place?' came her cool enquiry.

'Not at all.' He stepped inside without waiting to be asked, immediately removing his jacket then plucking aside the bow-tie. 'That's better.' He continued to undo the buttons at his neck as his eyes roved around the flat. 'Hmm...nice place,' he murmured, throwing her a smile then depositing his things on the nearest chair.

'I like it,' she said tightly. She closed the door and

turned to flick an uneasy glance around her recently refurbished flat.

Only a couple of lamps threw light into the living area and suddenly, she was reminded of what Sam had said about it the week before. 'Wow, sis, that's some room! Ve-ry sexy.' While Clare had laughed about such a description at the time, now, she started seeing her choice of furnishings with new eyes.

The white shag-pile rug was overly thick and felt luxurious beneath bare feet. The focal point of the room, a wide four-cushioned sofa, was lushly covered in velvet the colour of red wine. Two overstuffed armchairs were also velvet, one black, the other a burgundy and white stripe. Sensuous fabrics. Rich, flamboyant colours.

Only one painting hung on the stark white walls. It showed a man and a woman reclining on a rug under a tree, a picnic basket nearby. Clare had always found the scene relaxing, yet now, as Matt walked over to look at it, she had a totally different view. Suddenly it seemed that the couple's eyes were half-closed because of the drugged aftermath of making love and not due to a full lunch. She pictured them lying on that rug, oblivious to the groups of people in the background, oblivious to everything except each other.

'Rather an erotic painting, isn't it?' Matt commented as he turned slowly round to fix her with a thankfully bland look.

'I've never thought so,' she managed with an airy nonchalance.

Till now, she added privately, her eyes travelling down his handsome face, past a strong, tanned neck, into the swirl of dark hairs springing up from his chest.

She'd made it down to his waist before dragging her

eyes away and walking on wobbly knees to the walnut corner cabinet. With her back towards him she was able to suck in a few calming breaths and pull herself together before turning round. 'What would you like to drink?' she asked politely.

'Got any port?' He flopped down on the sofa and rubbed his forehead with a long, elegant finger.

Clare brought out a bottle of Samuel port as well as two fine crystal glasses. They tinkled as she set them down on the marble side-table nearest Matt, and it took all her control not to spill the liquid as she filled both glasses. Her enforced composure was such little protection against the sexual aura vibrating from this man. Resisting his attraction was like skating on thin ice, she fancied. One slip and she'd go under.

Those knowing blue eyes bored steadily into her while she hovered with the drinks and she was half expecting him to do something obvious like stroke her fingers when she handed him his glass. If he did, she feared she would spill the whole kit and caboodle into his lap.

He didn't.

Her own drink in hand, Clare proceeded to sit down on the other end of the sofa, straightening her dress over her knees. Once settled, and at a reasonable distance from her adversary, she felt better. A little stiff maybe, but at least able to lean back, sip her port, and hold his gaze without wavering.

He smiled lazily at her. 'Thank God tonight's over.'

'Surely you must be used to that sort of function by now?' she said drily. 'You should be able to go through the motions on automatic pilot.'

'Tonight was a little different.' He sipped his drink

and eyed her closely. 'Bangaratta has, to say the least, surprised me.'

'Really? I would have thought it was exactly as you'd imagined, balloons and all!'

He laughed. 'Funny you should say that. It was the first thing that struck me. The balloons!'

'I would have thought it was Flora in her red and pink dress.'

He shot her a startled glance but made no comment. Then he said the most amazing thing.

'You're still in *your* dress, I've noticed.'

Her mouth dropped open. My God! Had he expected her to slip into 'something more comfortable'? A black lace négligé perhaps? And why, damn it, did she find such an outrageous expectation so exciting?

He laughed and quaffed back half of the port. 'I dare say that sounded terrible.' He placed the glass back on the table. 'All I meant was that I can never wait to get out of these penguin suits. Don't women like to discard their finery as well?'

'Oh...' She just had to look down, terrified that her expression would give her away. 'Well, I haven't really had time and I'm not that uncomfortable.'

'You look uncomfortable.'

Her heard jerked up. 'Well, I'm not!' she retorted. There was a certain safety in anger.

Again he laughed. 'You do have a short fuse, Clare. Don't worry, you have nothing to fear from me. And don't deny what you've been thinking.'

That shook her. Surely he *couldn't* see right inside her mind.

'Bill told me what you said,' he added.

'Did he now?'

Matt grinned and picked up his port again. 'He thought it only fair to warn me.'

'And was I right?' The provocative words fairly tumbled from her mouth. 'Was this invitation for a drink together just a cover for an expected sexual rendezvous?'

The laughter died from his eyes, replaced by a puzzled frown. 'Do you want a truthful answer to that or not?'

'You said you admired honesty. In yourself, or only in others?'

'Both, I hope.' The blue eyes hardened as they swept over her. 'I'll make a bargain with you. I'll answer your question honestly if you answer mine first.'

A charge of adrenalin shot through Clare at the uncompromising ruthlessness in his eyes. He was looking at her in a way that chilled her soul, but at the same time aroused her body, and try as she might, all she wanted was more and more...

'Not the fairest of bargains, perhaps,' she countered, heart pounding, 'but I'm game.'

'Good. Then tell me... Is it me personally you dislike? Or all actors?'

'That's easily answered.' She sipped her drink, her grey eyes challenging him over the rim of her glass. 'Both.'

There was the minutest raising of an eyebrow. 'And might I request an explanation?'

'Aah...' Her smile was sardonic. 'That was not part of the bargain. Now you have to answer my question.'

'What was it again?' He poured himself a second port. 'I've forgotten the exact wording.'

'Liar!' she accused, thoroughly enjoying the battle of words. 'You, Matt Sheffield, would never forget words.

Or lines. You're just trying to embarrass me by making me say it.'

'Say what?'

'That it was sex you were expecting, not merely a drink.'

He fell irritatingly silent, savouring his port and giving her another of those disturbing looks.

'Well?' she prompted. 'Is that what you were expecting?'

'And I'm to be honest?'

'Of course.' A tingle shot up Clare's spine as she waited for his answer.

His gaze was unnervingly frank. 'I had no lecherous intentions when I asked to meet you for a drink. All I wanted was to get away and relax with someone who both interested and intrigued me. I thought I might find out why you seemed to like me one moment then despise me the next.' He leant back, crossing his ankles. 'Actually...I'm not in the habit of sleeping with a woman on such short acquaintance.'

His bluntness truly took the wind out of Clare's sails, making her feel horribly cheap, as though she had been the one to suggest sex.

'Of course,' he resumed, a mocking sound in his voice, 'I'm prepared to make an exception, in the circumstances.'

The breath zoomed back into her lungs, propelled by sheer anger. Or was it fright? She was getting out of her depth here. 'And what do you mean by that?'

'I mean...' he began swirling the drink in his glass '...that some women bring up the subject uppermost in their minds. If you're desperate to go to bed, I'm rather tempted to oblige.'

'Oh!' She jumped up, and several drops of port sloshed over the glass onto her beautiful rug. 'How dare you? Who do you think you are, saying such things? Brother, you've got a nerve. You asked to meet me for a drink, not the other way around.'

'You accepted,' he said quite calmly, 'believing it was for more than a drink.'

'Only because I wanted to show you that living in the backwoods didn't make a woman a pushover! I wanted to get up your hopes so that I could spit in your face!'

As soon as the ghastly words were out of her mouth she regretted them. She closed her eyes tight and a trembling sigh shook her body. 'Oh, God,' she rasped. 'God...'

He must have stood up, for he took the drink out of her hand. 'Have you got anything to sponge down this rug with?' he said, completely ignoring her outburst.

Her eyes flew open to find him standing in front of her, a tightly cold expression on his face. An agonised groan of dismay escaped her lips when she finally saw the state of her rug and she dashed for the sink. Snatching up a wet sponge, she flew back to the damage, got down on her knees and rubbed away at the offending stains. 'Oh, God!' she sobbed again, but not because of the rug.

'I think I'd best be going,' Matt said with a weary sigh.

'No...' She staggered to her feet and threw him a beseeching look. 'Please... I have to explain...'

'You don't have to. It's quite obvious that you overheard me talking to Bill earlier this evening and decided to teach me some sort of lesson. I must admit, though, that it was unfair of you to condemn me for being an actor this evening. Your performance has been exceptional. Just the right amount of coolness, then the flashes of interest. I even detected a hint of desire. Damned how you managed that! I take my hat off to you.'

'It wasn't like that.' She felt and sounded desperate. 'I...I did overhear you and I was angry. I thought you were belittling us. But later I...it wasn't...wasn't all acting.'

'No?' He was sceptical, with good reason. He took a step forward, his hands reaching out to close firmly over her upper arms. Even through the collar of her dress, her skin leapt at his touch. 'Then tell me what it was, then.'

Oh, lord, this was awful. Her heart was hammering wildly in her chest and her stomach was turning over and over. All she could do was shake her head dumbly.

'What in hell does that mean? You certainly weren't lost for words earlier.'

'Nothing... Nothing...' She tried to pull away from his disturbing touch but his fingers tightened, preventing her from breaking free.

'Tell me!' he ground out. 'And stop pulling away from me. You want me to touch you almost as much as I want to touch you, God damn you!'

She stared at him and what she saw, frightened her. She shook her head from side to side, eyes falling to the floor.

'You just won't admit it, will you?' One hand left her arm. It reached up to force her chin upwards so that she had to look at him. 'Is it because I'm actor? Do you think we're all liars? Egomaniacs? Incapable of true feelings? That's not true, Clare. I have feelings. I can be hurt. And you've hurt me tonight.'

'Matt...please...I didn't mean to...'

'No?' Anger turned those blue eyes to slate. 'I'm no fool, Clare. You had your mind made up before you even met me, well before you overheard that conversation. You wanted to hate me. I was a condemned man in your eyes. You sat there like that iceberg waiting for the Titanic, a mass of destruction lying beneath the surface. Well, I hit you, but you're the one who's going down, honey. I'm a bloody good swimmer.'

'But I don't hate you,' she blurted out. 'Not really. You...you reminded me of someone. Someone who hurt me once, very much.'

His sigh was deep, the tension in his bruising fingers draining away. 'Aah...so that's it...ah, yes, I see.'

'No...no, you don't see. You couldn't possibly see.' How could he ever see that she was terrified of these feelings exploding up through her body?

He reached down to pull the twisted sponge from her clenched fingers, throwing it away. And then his arms were winding around her and he was kissing her, slowly and surely, kissing her with an expertise not even the most sophisticated woman could resist.

Clare did not even try to resist. She couldn't. Her mouth flowered open beneath his, her immediate submission sending a groaning shudder through Matt's body. His hands wound up into her hair and he was pulling her head back, keeping her mouth open, thrusting his tongue deeper and deeper into its eager, compliant depths. With each thrust a hot dart of fire shot through Clare, racing up into her head where the blood began pounding in her temples like a jungle drumbeat.

A tortured moan struggled from her throat.

Immediately he drew back, a dazed questioning look in his eyes. Clearly, he had mistaken the sound for one of distress and Clare realised foggily that he was giving her the chance to stop. Don't think, her aroused senses screamed at her. Don't think! And for God's sake, don't stop!

Swiftly she pulled his mouth back down on to hers, winding her arms around his neck then pressing her throbbing breasts into his chest. Her own tongue slipped past his lips with a passion that would later astound her.

Somehow Matt's shirt was discarded and they made it over to the sofa. He sank down first, pulling her on top of him, their mouths still melded together. His hands left her hair to rove hotly over her back and the wild waves cascaded in a curtain over their faces. Clare's head began to spin from lack of breath and reluctantly, she pulled back to gasp briefly for air.

'Clare…lovely Clare,' he murmured, pushing back her hair and pressing light, fluttery kisses on her swollen lips. 'I want to make love to you. I'm going to make love to you…'

He sat up, taking her with him. 'Let's get this dress off.' He unzipped it in one expert moment, ignoring her strangled noise of protest. Good lord, what was she doing?

'No, Matt,' she finally rasped as his hands plucked away her bra. But her breasts broadcast her lie. They quivered under his touch, leapt taut into his palms, begged for his lips. 'No,' she croaked again, but he ignored her, and soon she didn't care. Naked desire charged through her veins, making her head spin and her body burn. When he stretched her out on the rug and started removing the last of her clothes she made no further protest. His hands on her bare flesh felt beautiful. *He* was beautiful.

He stopped so suddenly that she was left open-mouthed and panting.

'What is it?' she gasped. 'What's wrong? Why have you stopped?'

He was shaking his head. 'We can't, Clare. Not unless you have something here I can use...'

She stared up at him, the blood still roaring in her head.

'It's too risky these days, sweetheart,' he said regretfully. 'I'm sorry. I didn't mean to go this far. I lost my head for a while...'

Her eyes opened further. My God, he had lost *his* head for a while? Hers had been totally scrambled, as had her brains! Why hadn't she thought of protection herself? She hadn't been in Bangaratta that long that she didn't know the risks of casual sex.

It dazedly crossed her mind that there was a whole shopful of protection downstairs, but the thought slid away as quickly as it had come, those last two words echoing in her head. Casual sex. Casual sex. Casual sex.

And with a man she'd only met tonight.

Her self-disgust was immediate and violent, her flushed face grimacing as she rolled away from him and snatched up her clothes. She fairly ran into her bedroom and slammed the door shut, hugging her dress to her nakedness, shivering and shaking as she leant her back against the door.

But shutting the door didn't shut out the cold, hard reality of what she'd almost done. The truth kept infiltrating Clare's embattered senses and she could hardly believe any of it. Only Matt's common sense had saved her from possibly the second biggest mistake in her life.

Matt's firm knocking on the door made her spin away

from where she was still leaning against it. 'Go away,' she told him, her voice raw with emotion. 'Just go away.'

'Don't be so bloody stupid, Clare. I'm not going anywhere. Now put something on and get yourself out here. I want to talk to you.'

'No.'

'Clare... There is no lock on your bedroom door. I could just as easily come in. Make up your mind what you want to do.'

'I...I'll come out.'

'Good. Don't be long. It's getting damned late.'

His harsh attitude evoked a face-saving defiance in Clare. Who did he think he was, speaking to her like that? So what if he had more control and common sense than she had? Did that give him the right to order her around, to inflict his will on her?

If she came out it was because she wanted to, and only to show him she had not fallen apart, simply because he'd stopped making love to her.

Gathering every ounce of composure and courage she owned, she dragged on a warm dressing-gown, put a brush through her messed-up hair, then flung open the door. But the instant sight of a bare-chested Matt calmly slipping into his shirt brought back the potential sordidness of the situation, and her own ongoing vulnerability to the man.

He spun round at her groan, his intuitive blue eyes taking in her shattered face. 'Oh, honey,' he said, his face melting as he came over to draw her, unprotesting, back into his arms. 'It's not the end of the world,' he murmured, stroking her hair and her back. 'There'll be another time and another place, and I'll have all the protection in the world with me. I promise.'

She wrenched out of his embrace, wide eyes projecting her utter shock that he thought this was a mere hiccup in his sex life. 'There will not be another time,' she told him fiercely. 'Or another place, or another anything! Now I want you to leave, please.' She stepped back, wrapping the dressing-gown tightly around herself.

'What's the main problem, Clare?' he probed mercilessly. 'Are you appalled that you got so carried away so quickly? Or appalled that it was *me* you were getting carried away with?'

'I…I…' Her chin wobbled as tears flooded her eyes. God, now was she was going to make an even bigger fool of herself.

Once again he took her into his arms, and once again, she failed to protest.

'Tell me what's wrong?' he asked gently. 'Please…'

She glanced up through soggy lashes at the concerned blue eyes. He wasn't to blame. She would have liked to blame him. But she had known all along what type of man he was. Egotistical. Ruthless. A taker. Just like David.

'There's nothing wrong,' she muttered, pulling away again and walking over to the kitchen where she yanked a handful of tissues from the box on top of the refrigerator. She blew her nose and returned to find Matt drawing on his jacket.

'You know, Clare,' he said, then hesitated, shooting her a pensive glance, 'I did mean it when I said you were an exception to the rule. I don't make a habit of doing this sort of thing. I gather you don't either…from your after-shock.'

Her hand clenched tight around the tissues. 'No. No, I don't.'

'If you think I think you're cheap, Clare, nothing is further from the truth. I think you're a very special lady. A lady I'd like to get to know better.'

My God, she thought bitterly. Did he feel he *had* to say these things? She'd been a failed one-night stand, that was all. Tomorrow he would wing his way back to Sydney and his life playing Dr Adrian Archer, and she would never ever see him again.

Except on the television of course. Her weekly viewing of *Bush Doctor* would take on a different perspective after this. If she could bear to watch, that was...

'I have to go,' he said, and bent to give her a peck on the cheek. 'See you tomorrow,' he added unexpectedly.

'Tomorrow!' she gasped. 'I...I thought you'd be flying back to Sydney tomorrow.'

'I'm booked on the evening flight.' His smile was unsettling. 'Your mother kindly invited Bill and myself to Sunday dinner. Didn't you know?'

Clare's chest was being held in a vice. 'No.'

'I'm sure she's expecting you.'

'I...I go home for dinner every Sunday.'

'I'll see you there, then. And Clare...'

'Yes?'

'I think you're delicious...' He kissed her softly on the lips. Twice. 'See you tomorrow.' A short laugh followed. 'Make that today.'

He left. She watched him walk down the stairs and get in the car parked in the shadows. He waved briefly before driving off. She stared for a long time at the empty lane.

Finally, with slow, dazed movements, she turned. Her eyes moved across to the sofa, the dirty glasses, then finally to the painting. It seemed to mock her, reminding her cruelly of all she'd vowed earlier that evening. What a laugh! Words kept revolving in her head…words Matt had said. 'I don't think you're cheap… You're a very special lady… I think you're delicious…'

Charming words. Clever words. Complimentary words. Words designed to tantalise and seduce. Words to get her into his bed. Not words of love, however.

David had talked of love…incessantly.

Yet it took him quite a few dates to get her into bed, not one night.

Matt had got further in a couple of hours than David had over a couple of months. She wondered if this was due to Matt's skill at seduction, or her own frustration. She was twenty-seven years old now and hadn't made love for over two years. Yet she had liked making love, had looked for it almost as much as David, despite actual intercourse having often proven anticlimactic for her.

Clare doubted it would have been anticlimactic with Matt tonight. By the time he'd taken her clothes off she'd wanted him inside her so badly it had been frightening. After-shock, Matt had called her tears. He'd been right there. And she was *still* in shock. Why, in the end she'd been consumed with nothing but sheer unadulterated lust for Matt.

And he knew it.

Clare groaned as she pictured the next day at her mother's dinner-table, herself on tenterhooks, Matt looking over at her with coolly confident eyes and Bill smirking at her with a knowing smarminess.

Oh, God… The prospect was appalling. She had to find some way out of that dinner. She just had to!

CHAPTER FOUR

CLARE woke to bright sunshine flooding her bedroom. A bleary-eyed glance at the bedside clock showed twenty-five past eleven, at which she struggled out from under the quilt and staggered, still half asleep, to the bathroom.

Plunging into a steaming hot shower revived both her sluggish muscles *and* her memory. Oh, hell! Had it all really happened? Had it?

Of course it had! she told herself brutally.

She groaned her dismay a second time, fully aware that if it hadn't been for Matt's cool head the situation this morning could have been appalling, rather than just mortifying.

There was a large amount of gratitude mixed in with her feelings for him at that moment. Still some anger at his presumptions, as well as an ongoing rueful appreciation of his exceptional appeal. But she was extremely thankful for his ability to control himself instead of recklessly forging ahead, regardless of the consequences.

A lot of other men would have acted first, then thought afterwards, not the other way around. To give Matt a second credit, he'd also acted with surprising fortitude and forgiveness afterwards. Really, her behaviour all night had been deplorable. She had no idea why he would want to have anything further to do with her.

Clare reasoned that, since Matt *did* want to see her again today, this underlined his superficiality in matters of man-woman relationships. He was thinking of her as a potential sexual partner, not a woman he could fall in love with, or vice versa.

In retrospect, she found it surprising that someone like Matt did not carry condoms around with him all the time. David would never have been so unprepared, she recalled savagely. Cool, calculating David! Always one to take precautions, always counting the odds, never taking chances. Damn, why did she have to keep thinking about that bastard? He was past history.

Snapping off the water jets, she grabbed the nearest towel and began rubbing herself dry so forcefully that her skin looked like a beetroot. She glanced up into the bathroom mirror, saw the anger in her actions and stopped, sinking down on to the edge of the bath.

Her heart filled with misery and pain, and she might have subsided into tears if the phone hadn't begun to ring. Sighing, Clare wrapped the towel around herself and walked back into her bedroom. It would be her mother, she knew, wondering why she hadn't arrived at the house yet. She usually got there around eleven and helped with the lunch.

Little did her mother know that, today, Clare was not going to arrive at all.

'Hello, Mum,' she answered.

Agnes Pride's strident voice belted down the line. 'Where on earth are you, Clare? It's nearly noon and our guests have already arrived. Matt said you knew about his invitation to lunch. He said he mentioned it to you last night.'

Oh, God! Did that mean he'd admitted being in her flat so late? The thought of her mother's tactless questions made Clare doubly determined not to go. 'I was just about to ring you, Mum. I'm sorry, but there's something wrong with my car. I won't be able to make it.' If she'd claimed a headache, her mother could have told her to take an aspirin and get herself out there quick smart.

'Oh, botheration!' There was a mumble of voices in the background. 'Never mind,' her mother came back on the line cheerfully. 'Matt says he'll come and get you. He'll be there in twenty minutes. Be ready and wear a dress!'

'But, Mum…' Too late. She'd hung up.

'Damn, damn and double damn!' Clare swore. Wasn't that just like her mother? Never prepared to take no for an answer. As for Matt… She seethed as she thought of him as well. Didn't he have enough gumption to take a hint when he got one? Why couldn't he just accept that she didn't want to see him after what had happened?

It seemed he wasn't prepared to take no for an answer either, she thought viciously. Typical of men like him. Bloody typical!

Still, Clare placed the blame for this embarrassing situation mostly at the feet of her mother. The only reason she wanted her out there was so she could crow to her cronies about how their famous guest-of-honour was very taken with *her* daughter. Agnes knew nothing would come of it, knew that Clare didn't even *like* the man. It was just a case of one-upmanship over poor old Flora!

In a fury of frustration, Clare flounced into her bedroom and pulled on the most disreputable pair of jeans she owned. Not only outrageously tight but raggy around the edges. Then she dragged out the emerald-green silk blouse that her mother had once said didn't suit her. And finally she brushed her hair out till it cascaded down over her shoulders in a wild electric mane.

When she swept down the back steps and strode over to Matt's rented Mercedes nineteen minutes later, her rebellious mood had not abated, showing clearly in her angry stride and flashing eyes.

'Rather cruelled your plan, eh?' Matt mocked smilingly as she climbed in the passenger side.

She flicked a savage glance over to where he sat, looking disgustingly relaxed in washed-out grey jeans and a royal blue T-shirt.

'What plan?' she snapped, unprepared to be either polite or agreeable. The sooner he knew that there would be no repeat of last night's performance the better.

'Your plan to avoid me at all costs,' he ground out, no longer smiling.

'I don't know what you're talking about.'

'Oh, yes, you do, sweetheart,' he muttered, accelerating down the lane.

'I am not your sweetheart.'

'There's nothing wrong with your car, though, is there?' he accused and turned out on to the highway. 'You just didn't want to see me again.'

She gave no reply, staring blankly through the side window.

'God, but you're an impossible woman! Look... How about we pretend last night never happened? Will that make you happy? Though damn it all, if you were genuinely regretting it, you wouldn't be tormenting a poor guy now.'

Her head jerked around to glare at him. 'Don't talk in riddles! I'm doing nothing to you.'

'No?' He swerved the car around on to the river road

and flew along it. 'Just look at yourself. Tight jeans, no bra, hair looking as if you've just left your lover's bed. You're a tease, Clare. Probably the only reason you were so upset last night was because someone finally called your bluff!'

'My God, you're hateful! You know damned well I haven't dressed this way for your benefit.'

'Then why have you?'

'To make my mother mad!' she pronounced, sounding like a thwarted ten-year-old.

Matt laughed. 'Well, you've already done that, sweetheart, by not turning up. Yes, yes, I know… You're not my sweetheart… Yet.'

'Brother, have you got tickets on yourself! But what city slicker hasn't?'

'You'd know, I suppose.'

'Too right I would.'

'Had a few affairs, eh?'

'Not as many as you, Mr Wonderful. Your love-'em-and-leave-'em tactics are world-famous.'

'Don't tell me you actually get newspapers out this far?' he derided.

'We even have television as well,' she countered sarcastically. 'Next thing you know, some important big TV star will come out to visit us.'

Those blue eyes swept over her like an Arctic wind. 'If he did, at least he wouldn't have to bring any of his bedmates with him. Out here, they're laid on!'

She hit him. On his arm, his shoulder, his head. Over and over. Hit him for all the hurt that had been welling up inside her for years. And in doing so almost killed both of them. Matt lost control of the car and it skidded perilously close to the steep riverbank. 'Stop it, Clare…

Stop it!' he shouted at her as he struggled to right the car. Braking in the loose dirt was hazardous but he finally pulled the vehicle to a screeching halt at the side of the road.

They faced each other, eyes blazing, chests heaving. 'God, woman! You damned near killed us.'

This truth was slow in coming but it did come, and when it did, Clare slumped in the seat, shocked to the core. Shaking hands fluttered up to cover her face as she groaned.

'It's all right, Clare,' he said softly but made no attempt to touch her. 'It's all right…no harm done. A miss is as good as a mile.'

'It's not all right,' came the muffled cry.

'Don't be so hard on yourself. And stop taking life so seriously. If you do, it'll kill you.'

She lowered her hands and stared wide-eyed at him. Don't take life so seriously? Good grief, couldn't he see that the situation *was* serious? Last night she had almost given herself, totally and intimately, to a man she'd only just met. Her behaviour had been reckless and disgustingly cheap. She did not even have the excuse of being in love.

'Tell me what's really bothering you,' he went on frankly.

'I suppose I'm ashamed,' she admitted. 'Ashamed that I could have lost my head like that. I would have let you do…anything.'

She heard him suck the air in between his teeth, heard his own shock at this very shocking admission. She turned her head away, pressing her clenched fist against her quivering mouth. 'I…I don't know what came over me.'

'I doubt you would have let me do anything, Clare,' he said drily. 'The truth is you needed a man. I just happened to be there.'

'Don't say that!' she cried, spinning back. 'I can't believe that!'

'Can't or won't?' He smiled then, a very sexy smile. 'Not that I don't like the sound of your protest. It would be rather nice to think I was special to you.'

It was on the tip of her tongue to say, 'Yes, you are!' but she bit the words back. It would have been a lie... Wouldn't it?

'What? No avowal of love?'

She remained silent.

'Good. Now you've started being really honest with yourself. Even nice girls don't have to be in love to enjoy making love, Clare. I'm surprised it's taken you twenty-seven years to realise that. Now all you have to do is smile at your mother and we'll all have a nice day.' He fired the engine and moved off.

Clare sat there, stunned for a moment. But she supposed he was right. Just because she'd always equated making love with being in love, it didn't mean there weren't other alternatives to sexual behaviour. But it wasn't for her.

'What...what did you tell my mother?' she asked worriedly. 'About last night.'

'Absolutely nothing.'

'Then how did you explain my knowing about you coming today?'

'I just said I told you at the hall. After all, she extended the invitation before you left.'

'Oh...'

'Truce, then?' Matt asked with an encouraging smile.

She sighed. What was the point of continuing with this antagonism? 'Truce,' she muttered.

'We'll start again from scratch,' he said.

'If you like...'

'Good.' The smile became a grin. 'Miss Pride, may I present Mr Matt Sheffield? Hello, Mr Sheffield. What? You're an actor? God, how crass! Never mind, I'm prepared to overlook such an obvious failing for one social afternoon. And me? Well, I'm a chemist. You don't like lady chemists? Think they're prim and proper, narrow-minded bigots? Oh, well...one can't be perfect. As long as they've got sparkling eyes, gorgeous hair, long legs and firm...'

Her laughter drowned his last word.

'Do you know, Clare, that's the first time I've heard you laugh?' He flicked her a heart-catching look. 'You should do it more often.'

'There's Mum and Dad's drive,' she said, valiantly trying to ignore the way that look twisted her heart.

'What a pretty blouse, Clare,' her father complimented, coming round to help her out of the car. 'And I do so like your hair down.'

Dear Dad, she thought, as she kissed him on the cheek. Quiet, unassuming, he never gave offence and never disagreed with anyone, particularly his wife.

Agnes Pride swept down the front steps, done up to the nines. She gave Clare's clothes the once-over, her disapproving eyes telling it all. 'I was beginning to wonder where you'd got to,' she said. 'I thought maybe Matt had got lost.'

'Not with your splendid directions, Agnes,' he smiled, taking her elbow.

'Didn't Bill come?' Clare asked, hoping he hadn't.

'Mr Marshall's out the back,' her father put in. 'Helping Samantha.'

'Perhaps we should join them,' Agnes said, and with Matt on one arm and her husband off the other, steered the two men along the path that led to the back yard.

Clare brought up the rear, her stomach full of butterflies. She just knew the sort of look Bill Marshall would give her. She also wondered exactly what he was helping her sister with.

The Pride farm was not a real farm in the true sense of the word. It was a hobby farm. About thirty acres, the land rose gently to a knoll in the middle, where the old-style home was perched. Out the back, large tracts of mown grass sloped down to the river, and on this November afternoon the lawn was a mottle of dead winter grass and new spring growth.

Years ago, her father had made a splendid barbecue area near the back veranda, but it was rarely used. Agnes Pride didn't like 'charred' meat. So Clare was amazed to see the barbecue smoking away and an array of salads set out on a couple of outdoor tables. An aproned Bill was busy helping Sam turn the steaks on the grill, a can of beer in his spare hand.

'Just in the nick of time,' he said to the new arrival, looking at her with a blessedly bland expression. 'These steaks are done.'

'Go and bring out the plates please, Clare,' her mother ordered. 'You get the bread rolls, Samantha. Jim, open up the wine.'

Everyone followed their orders and lunch was promptly served.

Clare was grateful for once for her mother's garrulous nature. Agnes Pride never let the conversation slacken for a moment. There were no awkward silences and, thankfully, no smug looks from Bill. Maybe this was because Clare was seated between the two men, and she didn't ever have to really meet the agent's eyes. Not that she thought Matt would have told him anything. Not in so many words. At least she hoped he hadn't.

Once, Matt moved his thigh against Clare's. She shifted slightly away from him and quickly subdued her galloping heartbeat. But when a quiet hand closed over her right knee she almost died. She was occupied at the time, cutting her steak, so it was impossible to just drop the knife and fork without being obvious. The hand was actually roving upwards. Clare held her breath and turned slightly to give Matt a frosty smile. He raised his eyebrows and removed his hand.

The man was a menace, Clare conceded, not for the first time. He rode roughshod over her emotions, making her feel inadequate to control him. She had the awful suspicion that if ever they were alone again the same disastrous thing would happen as had the previous night. Yet, as he had warned, the next time he would be prepared. The sooner he left Bangaratta the better, she told herself repeatedly.

'Clare's mad about *Bush Doctor*,' Samantha announced as they were lingering over coffee. 'She won't miss it for love or money.'

Matt smiled. 'Is that so? I had no idea.'

Clare gave her sister a withering look. Sam turned up her nose in a gesture of defiance.

'I'm not such a fan myself,' she rattled on. 'Everyone in it's too old and boringly good.'

'Samantha!' her mother rebuked. 'Don't be rude.'

'I'm not being rude,' Samantha pointed out archly. 'I'm merely telling the truth.'

Clare had to bite her tongue to stop herself from laughing. Her mother was speechless for a moment also, perhaps recognising one of her favourite phrases coming out of the mouth of her teenage daughter. Samantha had the tone down pat also.

'There is a fine line, daughter,' Jim reproached gently, 'between telling the truth and being rude. Tact is a virtue all people should aspire to.'

Guilt consumed Clare as she thought of how rude she had been to Matt last night.

An awkward silence descended, broken when Bill cleared his throat and stood up. 'That was a lovely meal, Mrs Pride, but I have to return to the hotel to make some phone calls. Please, don't get up. I can see myself out. Matt, I'll come back at five. We can go straight from here to Dubbo airport.'

Once Bill had left, the women began clearing the table. Clare felt obliged to help her mother wash up but Samantha was despatched down to Lisa's place while Jim took Matt into his den to show him his stamp collections.

'What took you so long to get here?' Agnes asked Clare as soon as the men were out of earshot.

'Were we that long? I suppose Matt drove rather slowly. He's not familiar with the roads.'

'He seems to really like you, Clare. I don't know why you couldn't have worn a dress today. You looked quite lovely last night. I was so proud of you.'

Clare almost dropped the plate she was drying. Flustered by this belated and highly unexpected compliment, she was almost grateful when the men reappeared in the kitchen at that moment.

'How about taking Matt for a walk down to the river, Clare?' her father asked. 'He says he likes a walk after lunch. I'd take him, only my sciatica's playing up today.'

Clare gave Matt a sharp glance and wondered how he'd engineered her father's sciatica.

'Go on, Clare,' her mother urged. 'I can finish up here.'

Clare gave in, wiped her hands on the tea-towel and smiled sweetly at Matt. 'Let's go.'

He was barely out the back door before he said, 'Such a sweet smile. Was it a ''come into my parlour'' smile or a ''don't count your chickens before they hatch'' one?'

'Oh, Mr Sheffield, such cynicism! What happened to our truce?' This was the way to play it, she was sure. Light, yet lemony.

'The cold war was warmer than a truce with you,' he muttered.

'I didn't realise I'd been anything but polite at lunch.'

'Oh, you were polite all right. Chillingly so.'

'Just because I didn't return your sneaky little thigh-press under the table...'

He stopped suddenly. 'You noticed!'

'Oh, no-o! I missed it entirely. As I did your pawing up my leg. Would you mind keeping on walking? Mum will be watching.'

'Will she?' He caught up with her.

'Yes, I think she's harbouring hopes.'

'Really?'

'Not marital ones. She's no fool, my mother. I think she hopes I'll follow you to Sydney.'

'To become what?'

'Certainly not your nurse, Dr Archer.'

They were halfway down the hill by this time, out of sight of the house. Suddenly Matt took her hand and he was pulling her down the rest of the slope. He wouldn't let her stop till they reached the clump of trees on the riverbank, where he pushed her up against the shelter of a large trunk.

They faced each other, completely out of breath. His body blocked any hope of escape, his palms resting on the bark on either side of her face. His desire-filled gaze never left her in doubt what he intended doing. 'No, Matt,' she croaked, her stomach lurching.

'Yes, Clare, yes...' He kissed her lips, her nose, her eyelids. Sweeping back her hair, his mouth covered one ear, the tip of his tongue darting inside.

'No!' she cried, wrenching away.

He stared at her, eyes dilated. 'Why not?'

'Why not?' she repeated hoarsely. 'The fact that you ask why not is the very reason why not!'

'You're an experienced woman, Clare. You're not some shy virgin. So I repeat. Why not?'

'Because it isn't right!'

'Why not?'

'Because you don't love me.'

Exasperation catapulted into those bright blue eyes. 'So if I say I love you, everything would be all right?'

'Of course not! You wouldn't mean it.'

'How do you know I wouldn't mean it?'

'Oh, don't be ridiculous! As you just said, I'm not a naïve little virgin and I know you don't love me.'

His eyes narrowed. He lifted his chin, the action emphasising the stubborn set of his jaw. 'I won't quarrel with either of those statements,' he said curtly. 'But I don't see what difference that should make to adults. Virgins have never held any kind of attraction for me and as for being *in love*? I've never set much store by that particular state either. It's romanticised and overrated. Isn't liking, admiring, respecting and desiring just as important?'

The frustration went from his eyes as they caressed her face. One hand reached out to trace the line his gaze was following, across her forehead, down her cheek, encircling her mouth. 'I like you, Clare. I admire you. I respect you. I desire you,' he whispered, leaning close.

An answering desire licked along Clare's veins as her lips responded to his touch. Just in time did she pull herself up short. 'Do you?' she snapped, pushing him away again. 'I can't say I'm convinced of that. I think you're just feeding me a convenient line. Get this straight, Matt. I'm not going to let you have sex with me this afternoon. You can have a whole pocketful of condoms and the answer's still no.'

'I don't have any damned condoms with me,' he snapped. 'God, Clare, why must we always be arguing?'

'Because you don't listen. All you want is your own way. You forget that I know your type. I've come across it before.'

He stared at her, his eyes sharp. 'That's it, isn't it? I'm to be condemned for what some other man did. God, I'd like to kill that bastard!'

'No more than I!'

'Who was he?' Matt demanded. 'What was his name?'

She refused to answer.

'Was he an actor?' he probed savagely. 'He must have

been. Why else would you hate them so? Would I know him?'

'Just drop it, Matt. Please... It's all over and done with.'

'Like hell it is. It's still eating you up.'

'What if it is? What's it to you, besides spoiling one afternoon's entertainment?'

He gave her a long, searching look. 'Do you still love him?'

She swallowed convulsively. Did she? She'd spent so much time hating David that she'd never explored the possibility that she might still love him. 'Why should you care if I do or not?' she shot back. 'You don't believe in the term!'

'Bloody hell! What on earth am I going to do with you, woman?' He grabbed her hand, pulling her out from behind the tree. 'Come on, we're going back up. Now!'

'Why?' she asked shakily as he dragged her along.

'Because if we stay down here I don't know how I'm going to keep my hands off you.'

'You mean you'd hurt me?' she gasped.

He stopped and glared down at her. 'If you call making mad passionate love to you hurting you, then yes!'

The admission took Clare's breath away.

'But let me tell you something else, Miss Clare Pride,' he went on relentlessly. 'No matter what you think, I do care about you. And when this day is over you won't have heard the last of me. No sirree. You can't get rid of me as easily as that!'

CHAPTER FIVE

'CLARE. Phone for you. It's STD.'

Clare's head jerked up from the dispensary counter, her stomach turning over. Nearly a week had gone by and she'd heard nothing. No phone call. No letter. Nothing.

At first, she'd told herself she hadn't wanted Matt to contact her, despite his passionate avowal that he cared about her. But as the days passed with grinding slowness, and no word came, a deep disappointment had betrayed her true feelings. She did want to see him again, despite the danger and the futility of it all.

'I said it's STD,' Sally repeated, giving her still seated boss a frowning glance before putting the phone down and walking away to attend to a customer.

Clare almost tipped over her stool as she scrambled to her feet and walked hurriedly towards the receiver. She tried telling herself that just because it was an STD call it still didn't mean it was Matt. But every nerve-ending was telling her differently.

Even if it is him, an inner voice warned wisely, *don't make a fool of yourself!*

She slowed her step to a more leisurely pace, picking up the receiver with seeming nonchalance. 'Clare Pride.' In an effort to keep cool, her voice came out rather sharp.

An audible sigh wafted down the line. 'Bill Marshall here, Miss Pride. I received a call from Matt early this morning and he asked me to contact you. He's been on location this week and tried to call you last night but couldn't get an answer.'

Clare groaned. The one night in months that she'd gone out in the evening and that was the night Matt tried to call.

'I was playing tennis at a friend's place and didn't get home till late,' she found herself explaining before she realised she didn't have to explain anything. Certainly not to this man, or even to Matt.

'What about tonight?' Bill said in that annoyingly bland voice of his. 'Will you be home tonight?'

No way was Clare going to give the impression she was prepared to sit at home, waiting, just in case the famous Matt Sheffield decided to give her a call. 'I'm going out tonight as well,' she said crisply, at which Sally glanced round over her shoulder and frowned at her.

Luckily, their lone customer had just left the shop and there was no one else to overhear this conversation. The grapevine around Bangaratta was quick, and inclined to exaggerated speculation. If one of the old biddies had listened to this little exchange, in no time Clare Pride would be labelled a gadabout. Or worse. A *loose* woman.

'What time will you be leaving your flat?' Bill persisted.

'Eightish.'

'I'll tell Matt. Goodbye, Miss Pride.'

Clare's throat tightened as she realised that the call had been terminated before she even had a chance to ask for Matt's number in return.

But did she really want his number? What would she do if she had it? Ring him? And say what?

Why haven't you called me, you bastard? I watched that damned show again on Tuesday night, fantasised all through it then went to bed and dreamed the most disturbingly erotic dreams I have ever dreamed.

'Are you all right, Clare?'

Clare's eyes cleared to see Sally in front of her, looking concerned. When she realised she'd been standing there, holding a dead phone and muttering to herself, her embarrassment was extreme. She winced a quick smile and hung up.

'Men!' she said with exasperation in her voice, hoping that would help cover the multitude of questions that seemed to be hovering behind Sally's curious eyes.

Sally was twenty-three and married to a highly unsuccessful farmer. She was Clare's lone assistant in the shop, a bright girl who had a heart of gold but a small town's insatiable appetite for gossip. Clare was glad she had not once mentioned Matt's name on her end of the conversation. If she had, all would have been lost. Sally would surely have put two and two together and come up with five.

Actually, Clare had been waiting all week for someone to mention having seen Matt either arriving or leaving her flat in the dead of night. Luckily, both flats on either side of hers were used as storage areas, not residences, which meant she wasn't inflicted with any busybody neighbours. And the lane running behind had a high paling fence which blocked out the backyards and houses behind that.

But it never failed to amaze Clare how quickly Bangaratta got to know the ins and outs of everyone's personal lives. And how quickly they condemned. Her mother's assertion that they were a moral community was inspired more by fear of being found out, Clare believed, than by an innate wish to be good. Wife-beaters, adulterers and thieves got short shift around the area, as did layabouts and 'loose' women.

Clare had no intention of being labelled this last one on the strength of Matt Sheffield's transitory interest in her.

'What men?' Sally asked with eager eyes, underlining Clare's need to be careful.

'An old boyfriend of mine from Sydney,' she invented. 'I haven't set eyes on him for years, but he got the urge to call me last night and see how I was, then was put out because I wasn't home when he rang. How unreasonable can you get? Frankly, Sally, I don't want him pestering me, which is why I told him I was going out again tonight. I hope he got the hint.'

Understanding dawned on Sally's face. 'Oh, so you're not really going out tonight at all. For a minute there I thought you had some secret boyfriend I didn't know about.'

Clare laughed. 'Who, me?'

'Well, you did look gorgeous the other night. I wouldn't blame some guy going potty over you if he'd seen you looking the way you did. John couldn't stop staring at you all night.'

'I thought everybody spent all night staring at the guest-of-honour.'

'That was only the women. The men were glued to you! It's as well you don't look like that every day, Clare, or you'd have all the females around here being green-eyed with jealousy.'

'They only have to come in here and get a gander at

me today and they wouldn't be jealous. I've got bags under my eyes I could use for luggage!'

'You do look tired. Haven't you been sleeping properly?'

'Not really.' Hardly at all, thanks to Matt Sheffield. Or was it Dr Adrian Archer who kept her awake? Damn, but which one was it she was attracted to? The television character, or the man behind the mask. They had become as blended in her mind as they were in Mrs Brown's.

'Why don't you take a sleeping tablet?' Sally suggested.

'I don't want to get on that merry-go-round, thanks very much.'

Or any other merry-go-round, she thought with a jab of dismay. Getting mixed up with a man like Matt Sheffield, even temporarily, was like getting on a merry-go-round. It would go nowhere, and all she'd end up being was sick to the stomach. Sick at heart too, if she wasn't careful. The other night proved that forewarned didn't necessarily mean forearmed. She was very seriously attracted to the man. In her book, there wasn't much between being very seriously attracted and falling in love. It was a small step, but a step she didn't want to take.

Clare went back to work, vowing to make that plain to Matt tonight when he called. *If* he called, she amended cynically.

Her telephone rang shortly before seven that evening. Clare had been up in the flat for over a hour after closing up the shop and had been unable to do a darned thing. Her level of agitation had risen with each passing minute, so that when the phone finally rang, all the sensible resolve she had gathered during the day was obliterated, replaced by a rush of relieved happiness which had no agenda except racing into the bedroom in her eagerness to hear his voice again.

She swept up the receiver, saying a breathless, 'Yes?' as she pressed it to her ear.

'Clare? Is that you?'

It was a male voice all right. And a well loved one. But it was not Matt's.

Clare slumped down on the side of the bed, her disappointment acute. 'Yes, Dad. It's me.'

'So it is! Look, love, I meant to call you today but I forgot. Matt rang me at the bank yesterday wanting your flat phone number—it's not listed under your name. I didn't think you'd mind my giving it to him so I did. Did he ring?'

'Er...yes, he did,' she said. It was easier than explaining everything.

'He seems very keen on you, Clare. Do you think anything might come of it?'

'No, Dad, I don't, so please don't say anything to Mum. You haven't, have you?'

'I'm not that silly, love. Shame about Matt. I really liked him.'

'He's an actor, Dad.'

'So? What's that got to do with anything?'

She sighed. 'Nothing, I guess.'

'Don't judge a book by its cover, daughter. Must go. Dinner's on the table. See you Sunday. Be good.'

Clare shook her head, smiling at this last bit as she hung up. Being good in Bangaratta was easy. She was walking back through the living-room, wondering if Matt would really ring when there was a knock on the back door. Puzzled, she went to answer it, only to gasp in amazement. 'Matt!'

'The one and only.'

It certainly was, his handsome face smiling, those blue eyes twinkling, his nicely shaped body dressed with casual elegance in charcoal-grey trousers, blue shirt and a pale grey jacket.

'But…but…'

'I see you're not going out after all,' he interrupted, glancing down at her scruffy jeans, then back up to her unmade-up face and the spinsterish bun.

Her hands immediately itched to pull her hair free, to discard the functional white blouse in favour of something sexy. But then, she thought ruefully, setting dismayed grey eyes on those amused blue ones, Matt seemed to have that effect on her. He made her think of herself as a sex object, a woman waiting and wanting.

Amazing how the truth could infuriate.

'No,' she admitted coolly. 'It was called off.'

One eyebrow flicked upwards at her sudden change of tone. From flustered surprise to icy control. 'May I come in, then, for a while?' he asked.

'I suppose so.' She stepped back to let him stride inside. When he turned she gave him a coldly questioning look and said, 'I thought you were going to ring? Whatever are you doing here in person when you thought I was going out?'

His grin was decidedly mischievous. 'Would you believe I was in the neighbourhood?'

'Hardly,' came the dry reply.

'Would you believe I intended ringing but then, on the spur of the moment, I just had to see you?'

The words tugged at her heart but her once-bitten

brain was already in full gear. 'Really? I'm sure a phone call would have sufficed. Plane travel is awfully expensive. Or can good old Bill put this little junket on expenses?'

The smile faded. 'I see,' he ground out. 'Back to square one, is it?'

'Square one?'

'You know exactly what I'm talking about, Clare, and I'm not in the mood for word-games. For your information I took a normal flight, paid for out of my own pocket—as was the hire of the car. And I damned well expected a better welcome than this!'

'Oh?' She folded her arms and glared at him, grateful that he couldn't hear the way her heart was pounding. 'And why's that? I told you last Sunday I wasn't interested in having a casual affair with you. You should learn to listen better, Matt. No does mean no occasionally. I do realise you haven't heard that word often on female lips but that's hardly my fault, is it?'

'God, but you've got a tongue on you, woman.' He strode into the living-room and threw himself into an armchair. When their eyes met again she was astonished to see the smile was back.

'And what, pray tell,' she said sharply, 'do you find so amusing?'

'You, dear Clare. You.'

'Meaning?'

'Look, I refuse to indulge in your favourite pastime of throwing verbal darts. I'm here now and I intend staying for a while. One thing I'd like to know, though. Is there any other man or men in your life at the moment?'

'What on earth do you mean by "other"?' she snapped.

'Other than me, of course.' He was smiling broadly now.

Clare gave an exasperated sigh. He really was the most arrogant, infuriating man! 'You have a colossal hide,' she said, shaking her head. 'And an ego to match.'

'So I've been told,' he grinned, dragging off his jacket and tossing it over the back of the other armchair. 'Get me a cup of coffee like a good girl, would you? And please...spare me the feminist backchat. I'm not using you as a servant. I just don't know where the necessary utensils are.'

Clare spun away and flounced into the kitchen without a word. He had guessed her next reaction right down to a T. But if he thought he could bulldoze his way into her life and her bed, then he could think again! Clare was not one to make the same mistake twice. She'd underestimated Matt the other night, had underestimated her own sexuality as well. But she would not do so a second time.

Just don't let him touch you! came the rueful inner warning.

She took her time, making the coffee in a pot and arranging her best china coffee-cups on a tray, carrying it in with a charming smile on her face. 'Milk or cream?' she enquired sweetly, setting the tray down on the table between the two armchairs.

Matt's gaze narrowed suspiciously. 'Black,' he muttered. 'No sugar.'

'Watching our figure, are we?' Clare tripped off coyly.

The blue eyes relaxed only slightly. 'Who isn't these days?'

'I dare say you jog through your local park every morning too,' she said as she poured the coffee into the daintily flowered cups, the sarcasm hidden behind a soft voice. 'Or do you make it to Bondi Beach where all the other personalities gather?' She glanced up at him through her lashes and detected a wry smile hovering on his lips.

'Lady Jane, actually.' He leant over and reached to take the cup from her hand. 'Nothing like an invigorating pre-breakfast run along there. It really gets the blood going.'

With the mention of a well-known nudist beach, Clare realised then that he was mocking her right back. She grimaced ruefully and he laughed. 'You really have some awful preconceived ideas about me, haven't you? The truth is that I don't jog, I don't diet and I don't go to the gym twice a week. I work damned hard and, besides playing a spot of squash, I'm afraid my poor body gets little attention.'

Her gaze flicked over his 'poor' body. From what she could vividly recall it had felt lean and hard under her hands, with not an ounce of flab.

'I don't mind a game of squash myself,' she said, pouring her coffee and settling back in her chair with the cup balanced in her lap.

'You look athletic,' he commented and took a sip of the hot liquid.

'Why? Because I'm tall and thin?'

He lowered the cup and frowned. 'You're not thin. You're just right.'

Clare fell silent, her eyes staring blankly into her cup. She hated it when he started complimenting her. She was never sure if he was telling the truth or just flattering her for his own ends. In the short time she'd known him he had called her interesting, intriguing, desirable...and now just right. Each time he'd reaped the rewards. Firstly by capturing her own interest, despite her instinctive mistrust of his character, and now, by making her wonder if she was entirely wrong about him. Maybe he wasn't a clever Casanova, or a heartless charmer. Maybe he *did* have the odd sincere bone in his body.

But his being unmarried at the ripe old age of thirty-four spoke volumes. Matt clearly liked variety, preferring affairs to commitment. He was never going to offer her permanency. And yet…

Confusion reigned supreme in her heart as well as her mind. Whatever was she to do with this man? No way could she risk being so badly hurt again, but…

'What's wrong, Clare?' Matt asked softly. 'Why has my coming here upset you so much?'

She stared at him, cynical words tumbling round in her mind. Because I know why you've come. I know. I'm a challenge, and men like you can't resist a challenge. You have to win…at everything. Yet you don't care whom you hurt in the process. You don't care about the emotional wrecks you leave behind.

Still, it would be so easy to have an affair with you. God, so very easy…

She sighed and shook her head, her troubled gaze dropping to the floor.

His abrupt rising from the chair had her eyes jerking up in fear, but he merely packed the cups and saucers into the tray and started carrying it over to the sink. 'I'll help you wash up, if you like?' he offered, throwing an engaging smile back over one shoulder.

What could she say to that? Once again he had outmanoeuvred her. For the moment. 'OK,' she sighed, and stood up.

They washed up together in a silence which vibrated with tension. Clare was acutely aware of him standing next to her, drying up each item as soon as she placed it on the draining tray. She worried that it wouldn't be long before he made a physical pass and she wasn't sure how well she could handle that. The very thought sent a nervous tremor quivering through her.

Once the last teaspoon had been dried and the plug pulled out, Clare swung round to take the tea-towel from his long, lean fingers, using it as a sort of buffer between them. They said attack was the best defence, so she went on the attack.

'Right. Perhaps you'd like to tell me just why you are here, Matt? Surely you've got closer fish to fry.'

He leant back on the kitchen counter, palms down on the shiny surface, fingers splayed. He cocked his head slightly to one side and gave her a long, searching look. 'From what I can see I haven't even landed this fish yet.'

'No? With *that* bait?' Her gaze swept over his handsome, smiling face.

His smile took on a sardonic edge. 'Then it won't be long till you fall for me hook, line and sinker, will it?'

'I took a nibble,' she countered tartly. 'Not to my taste, I'm afraid.'

He drew himself upright, the blue eyes flashing angrily. 'You could have fooled me. You couldn't get enough the other night.'

The barb hit its mark but Clare was not about to give him the satisfaction of knowing it. 'Any port in a storm,' she flung back.

'Oh, don't be ridiculous, Clare. I can't stand this sparring back and forth. If you'd get rid of that chip on your shoulder you'd damned well see that I haven't come all this way just to seduce you. Damn it all, I want to talk to you, be with you.'

'I have not got a chip on my shoulder!' she denied hotly. 'And if I have, I've got just cause.'

'Oh, yes, that old chestnut again. Ah've been wronged.' His Southern drawl was perfect. 'Poor little ole me's been ruined. All men are varmints and I intend hatin' every one of them until the day ah die!' He threw up his hands then placed them squarely on his hips, glaring at her challengingly.

Clare froze. She should have been livid with his mockery. Absolutely riled to the core. Instead her chin was beginning to quiver and she was having difficulty containing the laughter that was bubbling up in her throat. She made a choking noise and whirled away, clutching the edge of the sink.

'Clare...' Unexpectedly tender hands closed over her arms. 'I'm sorry...I didn't mean to hurt you. Please... Don't cry, honey...'

The honey almost did it. She swallowed convulsively, struggling with her rising hysteria. He'd sounded so funny, like Rhett Butler himself from *Gone With The Wind.* She was dying to say 'Fiddledee-dee' right back at him then kiss him fair and square on the mouth.

She stayed as she was for a few moments, secretly savouring the touch of his hands and then, with a sigh, she turned. 'I'm sorry too,' she murmured thickly. Unfortunately, she could not control the wicked glints in her eyes.

'Clare Pride!' he reproached. 'You're nothing but a minx!'

She laughed. 'I couldn't help it. You appealed to my sense of humour.'

'You mean you have one?'

She went to give him a playful thump on the chest but he caught her hand, enclosing it in both of his. For a moment he held it close to his heart and then ever so slowly began to drag it up towards his lips. His eyes held hers as he uncurled each finger and finally pressed the open palm against his mouth. She caught her breath. The tip of his tongue grazed the tender skin, sending an electric shiver rocketing up her arm.

Her instinctive reaction was to pull her hand away but he pulled it back, and in doing so yanked her body against the length of his.

Fool, fool, she told herself. This is what he's so good at. This is what he came for, no matter how often he denies it. Pull away before it's too late.

His mouth was hot against her flesh. Her own skin was hot. Everything suddenly was hot. She swayed towards him, her eyes drowning in his. Her hand was being released as he was wrapping her into a close embrace. A suffocatingly close embrace. She could feel his thighs pressing into hers, pushing her back against the sink. There was no escape…no escape from his descending mouth.

'Please don't.'

Had those words really come out of her mouth? she wondered dazedly. That cool, calm command.

It must have, for he released her, a frustrated sigh betraying his annoyance. 'I was only going to kiss you,' he rasped. 'Nothing more.'

'So you say, Matt,' she went on with surprising determination. 'But I'm not into casual sex and there's no use pretending that adults can neck like teenagers and call a sensible halt at the appropriate moment. I know I can't.'

'Hmm.' He gave her a look from under half-closed lids. 'That much I've already gathered. You're a very sexy woman, Clare Pride.'

Another one of those cleverly seductive remarks, she thought, designed to undermine one's resolve. 'I like you, Matt. I can't help myself, despite having certain reservations. And yes, I'm physically attracted to you, as you well know. But that's not enough in my book to put aside some hard-learnt beliefs. If I let you make love to me...here...tonight...I'll regret it deeply. I'll become emotionally involved with you, and before I know it I will probably fall for you hook, line and sinker. I can't do that to myself twice. I won't!'

'You are presuming, of course,' Matt said quietly, 'that I will ultimately reject you. That I will throw you aside when I tire of you.'

'Won't you?'

He frowned and leant back on the bench behind him. 'I would like to think I wouldn't hurt anyone deliberately. Or use them without their wishing to be used. I was hoping we could be friends, Clare. And yes, maybe lovers. I admit I was hoping we could meet each other's sexual needs.'

'God! Meet each other's sexual needs.' Her top lip curled with distaste. 'Do you know how ghastly that sounds?'

He was staring at her, long and hard. A host of emotions passed through his eyes, not the least of which was a grudging admiration. Finally, he levered himself away from the bench and bent to kiss her lightly on the lips. Then he drew back, a serious expression on his face.

'Yes, Clare,' he said. 'Yes, I do know how ghastly that sounds.'

'Then don't expect it of me,' she whispered raggedly.

He fell silent for a few seconds then said, 'Perhaps I should take the easy way out. Say that I love you.'

She didn't even bother to stifle the derisive snort. 'You'd be lying and I'd despise you.'

'Hmm.' He continued to regard her with those penetrating blue eyes. Then suddenly he grabbed her arm and began pulling her towards the door. 'Come on. We're going out.'

'What?' He was already propelling her towards the door. 'I can't go out like this. I'm a mess.'

'You look fine to me.'

She stood her ground. 'I look terrible.'

He gave her a stern look. 'Perhaps that's just as well, then, isn't it? After all, if I'm to have a platonic relationship with a woman, it might as well be with one who looks completely sexless.'

Clare did not take offence. She had the oddest feeling that Matt had subtly changed his plan of attack. She wasn't sure yet what his new ploy was but she would work it out, eventually. 'All right,' she agreed. 'Don't forget your jacket. Where are we off to? Oh, and Matt, would you mind putting a paper bag over your face? You're much too good-looking for my peace of mind.'

For a split-second he was startled into silence, and then laughed. 'OK, OK, go and change, but be quick. We're going out to dinner. Not around here, of course. I spotted a motel just this side of Dubbo which had a small restaurant attached. Wouldn't want it getting round Bangaratta that you're a fallen woman.'

Clare laughed. 'The word is ''loose'' around here. But what makes you say that being seen with you makes me that?' she threw over her shoulder as she hurried to her room.

'God! Haven't you heard? All actors are the very devil with women. Lechers, seducers, downright cads!'

'True, Matt,' she muttered under her breath as she closed her bedroom door. 'Too true.'

CHAPTER SIX

'I LIKE you in pants,' Matt said when she reappeared, dressed in a green trouser suit with slightly flared bottoms and a cropped jacket with silver buttons. 'And if you make a smart crack back at me about that, I'll strangle you.'

Clare had to laugh. 'I wouldn't dare touch that one with a bargepole.'

'Lord knows how it came out of my mouth in the first place. Man must be going mad.'

'You and me both,' she muttered under her breath.

'I heard that,' he pounced. 'Now listen here, madam. I don't want to hear any more of your cynical preconceived ideas about me this evening. We're going to go out and have a pleasant time together. I want to see nothing on that lovely mouth of yours but sweet smiles. And you can keep that *not* so lovely tongue of yours silent unless you have something equally sweet to say. In the words of my dear departed Gran...if you can't say something nice, don't say anything at all!'

'Mmm. This could turn out to be a very quiet evening.'

'It certainly will if you keep that up,' he warned. 'Because every time you come out with one of those little sourpuss gems, I'm going to kiss you.'

'Promises, promises.'

His blue eyes suddenly narrowed on her mouth and

Clare's stomach churned. What was the matter with her, goading him like this?

'Be careful, Clare,' he said in a deceptively calm voice. Deceptive because she could see the steely glitter within his darkened gaze. 'Or you might get what you really want.'

'And what is that?' she asked shakily.

His smile was cool and calculating, yet at the same time quite cryptic. Clare tried to glimpse the man behind the mask but, try as she might, she could see absolutely nothing. This was a man who was a master at hiding his soul, at revealing nothing of his real self to the public at large, and herself in particular.

It reminded Clare forcefully of the role women played in Matt Sheffield's private life. They came and they went.

There was only one thing she was sure of. Before they went, they had all tasted the transitory delights of his bed. Or wherever he chose to make love to them.

Thinking about Matt making love to her undermined Clare's resolve to keep him firmly at bay. Behind her very sensible decision not to become involved with him, she desperately wanted to know what it would feel like to lie in his arms, to have his body thrusting deep into hers. She just knew it would take her to a peak of physical pleasure the like of which she had never known before. Just thinking about it was making her flesh tingle and her nerve-endings sing.

'Let's go.'

His cold command jolted her out of her sexual fantasy, a guilty blush flushing her cheeks. Sweeping up her keys and bag from the kitchen counter, she waved him through the back door ahead of her, locking up with irritatingly fumbling fingers before following him carefully in her high heels down the steep wooden staircase.

His hire car was a sleek blue Fairlane with grey upholstery which smelt of pine air-freshener. Matt saw her gallantly into the passenger seat before striding round to slide in behind the wheel. Once seated, he covered his eyes with a pair of wraparound sunglasses—despite the sun's having sunk behind the hills—then carefully checked the rear-view and side mirrors before driving down the lane, at the end of which he stopped again, waiting till there was no passing traffic before he proceeded out into the street.

The whole scenario irritated her.

'Frightened you might be seen with me?' she asked waspishly.

'I prefer to be unobtrusive,' came his smooth reply. 'I would think so would you, unless you want to be splashed across one of next week's gossip rags as Matt Sheffield's latest love interest. I've only got to stand next to a presentable-looking woman in the queue in the supermarket and I'm having a red-hot affair with her.'

'Are you saying the various reports on your private life are spurious and inaccurate?'

His sidewards smile was wry. 'I'm saying they are inclined to exaggerate.'

'So some of those women *have* graced your bedroom?'

'Good God, no. Let a woman into your bedroom and she's likely to think she belongs there. I usually go to hers,' he added drily. 'Or an emotionally neutral territory...like a motel.'

Clare suddenly remembered he was taking *her* to dinner at a restaurant attached to a motel.

His laughter brought her eyes snapping round.

'You should see your face. Come now, Clare, don't bother denying it. I said exactly what you expected to hear.'

Clare bristled with indignation. 'Maybe, but you really are a bastard where women are concerned, aren't you?'

'No. I am not.'

She made a scoffing sound.

'My dear Clare, I have never promised what I can't deliver, and I've always delivered what I *did* promise.'

'And would you like to explain all that? What is it that you can't deliver and never promise? And what is that you do promise, and always deliver?'

'I have never promised love or total commitment. I do promise to satisfy a woman's sexual needs. It's as simple as that. Of course, that latter arrangement doesn't appeal to you so maybe I'll be forced to reassess where you're concerned.'

Didn't appeal to her? My God, if he could see inside her right now he would find that her heart was going like a threshing machine and her blood was near to evaporating with the heat of her desire. How she managed to keep a cool face and a cool voice she would never know.

'As I said before, I do not indulge in casual sex, or casual affairs.'

'What if I promise not to be casual? What if I promise to take our affair very seriously indeed?'

'Meaning?'

'Meaning you will be the only woman in my life, utterly and exclusively.'

'My God, am I supposed to be grateful for that?'

'I was hoping you might be.'

She was still shaking her head in amazement at this

truly amazing statement when they came round a corner and a blaze of flashing lights ahead dazzled them both.

Matt immediately slowed right down. 'Looks as if there's been an accident,' he said thoughtfully as they approached.

Only one car involved, Clare quickly realised. By the skid marks it looked as if it had been speeding round the corner, lost control, careered off the road and slammed into a tree. Already the police and ambulance had arrived, with several more cars parked around. Clare was relieved to see she didn't recognise the car.

'No point in stopping,' she told Matt when he began pulling over to the side of the road fifty metres past the scene.

'There might be something I can do,' came his rather arrogant-sounding reply.

It got Clare's goat. 'For pity's sake, Matt, you'll only be in the way. You're not a real doctor, you know.'

Matt gave her a penetrating look before undoing his seatbelt. 'You'd be surprised what I've picked up on the set,' he said coldly. 'So if you don't mind, I'll just check and see if I can be of any assistance before we go on our merry way.'

Clare felt totally ashamed of herself as Matt stalked off. She shouldn't have said what she'd said. It had been most uncalled for.

He was gone several minutes, only returning after the ambulance took off, its siren blaring.

'Matt, I'm sorry,' she said straight away. 'I was very rude. Please forgive me.'

'What?' he said distractedly.

'I said I was sorry for saying what I did. I...' She broke off when Matt took off his sunglasses and she saw the look in his eyes. 'My God, Matt, what's wrong? You look ghastly!'

'The driver's dead,' he said abruptly.

Clare was stunned. 'But...but the car didn't look that bad.'

'His head must have smashed into the steering-wheel. His neck was broken. And before you say it, Clare, I'm well aware people do die in real life.'

Her hand came over to rest both comfortingly and apologetically on his knee. 'Yes, of course you are.'

His glance was sharp. 'Don't patronise me.'

'I...I wasn't!'

'Oh, yes, you were. Poor pretend Dr Archer, going green around the gills when he comes across a *real* accident and *real* blood. That's what you're thinking, isn't it?'

'No!'

His scoffing sound told her he didn't believe her.

'Matt, I said I was sorry and I am. I really wasn't patronising you. Do you think I would have felt any better if I'd seen what you've just seen? I also think it was very decent of you to stop and try to help. Who knew? You might have been able to do something.'

He was frowning hard, as though he was trying to make up his mind about something. An odd shudder ran through him and he began shaking his head from side to side.

'Matt, speak to me,' she begged. 'I can't stand seeing you like this.'

He looked over at her, a grim smile curving his mouth. 'I can't stand seeing *me* like this, either.' He reached out then and laid a heartbreakingly tender hand around her cheek. 'You really are a special lady, Clare Pride, and

I'd like to be able to promise you more than I usually do, but I'm afraid that's not possible. Not yet, anyway.'

She leant her head into his hand, savouring its warmth and gentleness. 'I...I haven't asked you to promise anything...'

'Then you'll let me take you to bed tonight?'

Clare's head jerked upright, and his hand dropped away with a sigh.

'I didn't think so,' he said ruefully.

Clare bit back the temptation to change her mind on that score. If she didn't look after her own happiness, who would? 'Look, Matt,' she said sensibly, 'I can appreciate that your present lifestyle is hardly suited to commitment, but I'm at a point in *my* life where that's what I want. I admit I'm madly attracted to you and I would like to go to bed with you. But as I said earlier, if I do, I might fall in love with you, and then I'll want more than the occasional night in bed. You've been honest enough not to promise what you can't deliver, so let me be equally honest back. I don't want to waste my time having an affair with you, and I certainly don't want to risk being hurt again like I was before.'

'Mmm. Methinks there's a chap somewhere down in Sydney whom I'd like to hang, draw and quarter. Are you sure you don't want to tell me about him?'

'No.'

'Why not?'

'Why should I lay my soul bare to a man who's going to be gone from my life after tonight?'

'What makes you so sure I will be?'

Her smile carried a cynical edge. 'When you don't get what you came for, Matt, you won't be back. It's too far to come, especially when there are plenty of pretty young things in Sydney, just panting to meet your sexual needs. You do seem to prefer young, from what I've seen.'

'Don't believe all you read in the tabloids. Besides, maybe my tastes have matured lately.'

'And maybe the earth is flat,' she said drily.

He laughed. 'You don't know me very well, Clare. If you did, you wouldn't challenge me so.' He leant forward and restarted the engine. 'Time to go on to dinner, I think. I'm beginning to feel very hungry. And no, there is no double meaning in that remark. I'm going to do my level best to play the gentleman tonight, dear Clare. But don't rely on that in future. Believe me when I tell you that acting does not always come naturally to me.'

The flowers arrived the next morning at the most inopportune moment. Mrs Brown was in the shop, as was Flora, both of whom viewed the arrival of the two dozen red roses with narrow-eyed suspicion. What on earth had Clare Pride been doing to deserve such an extravagant gesture? their expressions seemed to say.

Clare's heart fluttered as she took them from the delivery boy. They had to be from Matt. He'd dropped her off last night after dinner with a disappointingly platonic peck on the cheek but a firm promise to be in touch, his parting words being, 'I'm not a man to give up easily, Clare.'

The flowers were obviously his first ploy in his ongoing plan to seduce her. He probably thought they were the right move. What he didn't realise, however, was the speculation and possible embarrassment they would cause her around Bangaratta. The local florist was a notorious old gossip and with her whisperings Clare would definitely soon be considered a 'loose' woman, with everyone in town keeping their eagle eyes open to discover the identity of her mystery lover.

Clare cringed to think what Matt might have written on the note. Hopefully nothing like, 'Thank you so much for the wonderful evening.' The florist, and Bangaratta, would do wonders with material like that!

Fortunately, the note said no such thing, only a highly non-committal 'To a lovely lady.' Neither had Matt signed it. Nevertheless, Clare was wondering how to answer the inevitable questions she could see surfacing in the two ladies in the shop when suddenly her little white lie of the other day came unexpectedly to her rescue.

'They're from him, aren't they?' Sally said. 'That pain in the neck who called you yesterday.'

Clare hid her relief behind a weary sigh, handing the note over to an eager Sally. 'I guess he didn't get the message,' she said with just the right amount of exasperation. 'He contacted me again last night, you know. I just don't know what to do.'

'Are you having problems with some man, Clare?' Flora asked, her eyes bright with curiosity despite trying to sound shocked.

Clare didn't have to explain further, Sally was only too happy to do it for her.

'There's this old boyfriend Clare knew years ago in Sydney,' she informed the two wide-eyed customers. 'Out of the blue he's starting ringing her up again, and now he's sent her flowers. Next thing you know, Clare, he'll be on your doorstep!'

He's already done that, Clare thought with private amusement, while struggling to keep her face suitably worried-looking.

'You poor thing!' Flora exclaimed.

'He must be rich,' Mrs Brown murmured, 'to send such expensive flowers.'

'Is he rich, Clare?' Flora asked.

'Filthy rich.'

'Then what's wrong with him?' Mrs Brown put in, frowning her confusion. 'Is he ugly?'

'No, he's very handsome.'

'He's not married, is he?' Sally joined in worriedly.

'No, he's not married,' Clare answered.

'So what's wrong with him?' Mrs Brown persisted.

'Handsome and rich does not always make for a perfect life partner,' Clare told everyone, recognising the black irony in that. 'I guess I just wasn't firm enough last night. I'll make sure next time that he gets the message.'

Which might be a damned good idea, she added privately. But you won't do it, will you, you coward? You'll coo and gush as much as Mrs Brown and Flora did over the man, then let him run rings around you.

She looked at the roses and felt her insides go to mush. Oh, hell…

They looked glorious in her living area, the deep red petals a perfect foil for the white rug. Clare could not stop looking at them, touching them. The only thought that spoiled her pleasure was that Bill might have ordered them and not Matt. She had a mental picture of Matt calling his agent and saying, 'Send Clare some flowers, would you? A message? God, I can't think now. I'm too busy. Surely you can come up with something appropriate.'

She tried to dismiss the idea as unworthy but still, it persisted. Perhaps he even charged them to 'expenses'.

Lord! Now she was getting paranoid, allowing her cynicism to flavour everything. The man had sent her flowers, hadn't he? Why couldn't she just accept it as the nice gesture it was?

Because it wasn't a nice gesture, and she knew it. It was move one in a chess-game where Matt hoped to checkmate her. Or should she say, *mate* her? Clare knew she should be angry, but already she could feel herself weakening.

The phone disturbed her mental war and she moved reluctantly to answer it, groaning at the thought that it might be her mother. It wasn't past the Bangaratta grape vine to have reached the Pride farm by now. It was almost five, six hours since they'd been delivered.

'Hello. Clare Pride here.'

'Clare… How lovely to hear your voice. Did you get my flowers? I wasn't sure if Bangaratta had a florist but Interflora assured me there was one.'

Clare's pulse went into overdrive. 'They're…they're beautiful.'

'Red roses?'

'Yes, masses of them.'

'Ah…good. I specifically asked for red roses. I thought how perfect they'd look against your rug and sofa.'

'You…you did?'

'Sure did. Only the best for my best girl.'

Clare's heart flipped over with pleasure, then again with dismay. 'I wish you wouldn't say things like that.'

'Why not? It's true. You're the bestest girl I've ever met. *And* the most fascinating. I can't think of anything else but you. My mother blathered on to me over lunch today and I didn't hear a single word. My mind was a million miles away. With you...'

Clare gave a dry laugh. 'I'm not that far away.'

'Might as well be. God, I miss you, Clare. I wish you were here, with me. I wish I could hold you and kiss you and...'

'Matt, stop it!'

'I know, I know. But it's so tempting to say whatever I want to say when you're safely where you are and I *can't* touch you. It practically killed me, leaving you last night. I wanted to take you in my arms and never let you go.'

Clare gulped. 'Please don't...'

'All's fair in love and war, my darling.'

And which is this? she agonised. Love or war? It had to be the latter, since Matt didn't believe in love. The battle of the sexes, with sex as the prize!

'But you're not fighting fair at all,' she said shakily.

'I can't afford to. Not when the enemy is so elusive, yet so damned desirable. I'm not going to give up, Clare, till you give in. I don't care how long it takes.'

Oh, God, she thought. And how long will it be, at the rate my heart is going, before I'm begging him to make love to me?

'Somehow I don't see you being that patient,' she muttered.

'I never said I was patient. I'm going to pull out all the stops to persuade you.'

'Which is something you're very good at, isn't it?'

'Some people *like* to be persuaded. Not everyone is good at making decisions or choices.'

Her laughter was self-mocking. 'You remind me of

Henry Ford, saying you can have any colour car you like, as long as it's black.'

'Meaning?'

'I get the feeling that you won't give me any choices either.'

'I can't imagine anyone swaying you, Clare Pride. You're the proverbial brick wall.'

'And you're Wheelan the Wrecker.'

A low rumble of sexy laughter caressed her ear. 'I've been called a lot of names in my life but never that. Look, Clare, I'd dearly love to talk to you all afternoon but I'm supposed to be co-hosting this do, and people will be arriving soon.'

'What do is that?'

'My one and only sister's on the brink of becoming engaged. We're meeting the prospective man of the moment under the cover of a cocktail party this evening. I'll ring you later, OK?'

'Couldn't you give me a number where I can ring you?' she asked quite reasonably.

The delay in his answering roused her habitual mistrust. Did he want to keep their friendship a secret, or something? 'I suppose I can give you this number, if you like, but I'm not here that often. I don't live here.'

'Then where do you live?'

'Here, there and everywhere at the moment. I'm rarely in the same place two days running. Don't worry, darling, I won't leave you in the lurch.'

'Matt?'

'Yes?'

'Please don't call me darling.'

She heard him sigh. 'Why not?'

'It...it doesn't feel right.'

'Only a term for lovers, eh?'

'Something like that.'

'God, woman, you're hard.'

'I know.'

'But not as hard as all that,' he said softly, making her go all squishy inside. 'I have to go now, Clare, but every time you look at those roses, think of me, will you?' He hung up.

Her hand trembled as she returned the phone to its cradle. He was so right, she worried. So damned right! Where he was concerned she was anything but hard. He made her glow inside. He made her happy. He made her feel dangerously alive. And he damned well knew it! He was going to play a waiting game, wearing down her resistance till he got what he wanted.

To hold her, kiss, make love to her…

Somewhere, down deep, some long-buried emotion stirred. Again it moved, crying to get out, to be allowed once more to rule both her heart and her head. If she gave it free rein she wouldn't have to control her impulses. What a seductive thought! She could give in to them, then later excuse all in the name of…

Carefully, forcefully, Clare pushed it back, locking it up behind that protective wall she'd been building for such a long time. The effort was considerable, twisting at her insides and leaving in its wake a vast emptiness. But once achieved, a feeling of pride salved some of the misery. Satisfied with this small victory, she walked back into the living-room.

She stopped dead, a groan torn from her lips as two dozen red roses sent their silent, seductive message.

* * *

For nearly two weeks Matt rang her every night. Sometimes at a respectable hour. Sometimes late at night. And as if aware of her troubled mind, he no longer tried to make verbal love to her on the phone. They talked about the most mundane things and gradually Clare found that his nightly call became the most important thing in her life.

He was right about his never being in the same place two days running. He rang her from lots of different places. A couple of times from a unit in Kirribilli that was his base in Sydney but which he rarely seemed to use. Mostly he was on location, staying in various hotels, motels and caravan parks all over Australia. Dr Archer was a type of travelling doctor, working as a locum in a different country town every week, having a different and completely self-contained adventure in each episode.

The show aired forty weeks of the year, so Matt's schedule was gruelling and hectic. It was difficult, he told her, having to be in a certain place at a certain time when he was at the whim of others.

It was no wonder that actors' marriages broke up, Clare conceded. They would never be home. Matt was wise, in a way, to have remained single. When she mentioned this one night, he voiced the opinion that a husband and father had a responsibility to be home when needed, not flitting around the country.

She rather suspected he was talking about his own senator father as well when he said this, and she'd been moved by the underlying hurt she'd heard in his voice. It was widely accepted that politicians' wives and families suffered at the hands of their careers, and, where before she'd cynically dismissed this as the price they had to pay for their ambitions, Clare saw now this was a very harsh approach.

Suddenly, she found herself gaining a little more insight, and human pity. She realised that nothing was as cut and dried as that, and there was a lot of grey in every situation. Still, it would never be her cup of tea, having her husband flitting around, putting his work before home and hearth, living and breathing material success.

And with this realisation came more unease to add to her already unsettled state of mind. Just what was she doing, looking forward to Matt's call every night with increasing reliance, not being able to sleep till he had rung? Hadn't she learnt from bitter experience what became of a woman who fell in love with such a selfishly ambitious man? And if she was to stop that happening she had to put an end to these emotional crumbs he was throwing her.

So when Matt had the temerity to ring her close to midnight that evening—he'd been doing some night shooting—Clare had worked herself up into an irascible frame of mind.

'Matt, you do realise it's very late?' she snapped.

'Well, yes…but I didn't think you'd mind.'

'But I do mind. I have to work tomorrow and Friday's always a particularly busy day. I need my sleep.'

'I'm sorry, darling. It was thoughtless of me, but I do so like talking to you last thing at night. I don't seem to be able to sleep properly without hearing your voice.'

His words made her feel awful and wonderful at the same time. Oh, Matt, why are you doing this to me? 'I thought I told you not to call me darling,' she said sharply. 'And if you want someone to talk to in the middle of the night, then get yourself a teddy-bear!'

'I think I'd rather have a wife.'

Clare sucked in a shocked breath. 'You...you told me actors shouldn't get married. Or politicians!'

'Quite right.'

'What the hell are you playing at, Matt? Don't try to con me. You have no intention of getting married at all, let alone to me.'

'Certainly not while I'm doing this series. But things can change.'

'How?'

'Dr Adrian Archer might get killed off...'

'In a pig's ear. Tell me the truth, Matt. What's all this about? Is this just another ploy to get me into bed?'

He became suddenly serious, and disturbingly unsure. 'No...I don't think so. But if you went to bed with me I might be able to see things a little more clearly. It would get the sex part out of the way. Sex does have a way of colouring what a man might think is the truth.'

'Which is?'

He sighed. 'Now that's surely a difficult question. Hard to pin down...or to answer...I don't want to be premature. I also don't want to say anything that would have you running in the opposite direction so hard and fast that I'd need a trace to find you.'

'Matt, I don't know what you're talking about. You're making my head spin!'

He chuckled. 'You have the same effect on me, sweetheart. I've been going round in circles since the first second I set eyes on you, walking towards me in that blue dress.'

Dismay curled around her heart. What had Sally said about her in that dress that night? Was Matt suffering from nothing more substantial than an intense case of lust? He'd more or less suggested that his feelings for her might only be sexual, that if he slept with her his focus might clear. And, if she was strictly honest with herself, she'd suspected as much all along. He desired her, that was all. Nothing more, nothing less. All the rest were just trappings to gain that end.

She felt suddenly miserable and it annoyed her. She'd asked for the truth, hadn't she?

'Matt…'

'Yes?'

'I don't think you should ring me again.'

'Why ever not?'

'You're screwing up my life!'

'How?'

'I…I can't sleep till you ring me. I can't think of anything else but you and…and sex.'

'I recognise the symptoms,' he said drily. 'So what are you going to do about it?'

'What am *I* going to do about it?'

'Yes, *you*. I promised to give you the whip hand. How long do you think you can put up with climbing the walls?'

'Not…not long…'

'Well? Will you meet me somewhere next weekend?'

'Next weekend?' she repeated weakly.

'Yes, the weekend of the thirtieth. Can you get someone to fill in for you on that Saturday?'

'I suppose I can.'

'Good.'

'What…what did you have in mind?'

'I have an idea but I'll have to talk to the people concerned first. I'll let you know tomorrow night.'

She let out a shuddering sigh, which was a combination of surrender and relief. 'All right,' she whispered.

'God, Clare. I can't wait.'

'Me neither.'

His groan sounded tortured, and it sent everything inside Clare squeezing tight.

'I'd better go,' he went on gruffly. 'Now don't forget. Don't line anything up for that weekend. Rain, hail or shine, we're going to spend it together!'

CHAPTER SEVEN

CLARE was speeding. Nervous anticipation, she told herself, but she kept her foot down. The clock on the dashboard said six-thirty. She'd been driving since five thirty-five, not stopping for anything, and by her calculations should arrive at her destination shortly after seven-thirty. Fortunately with daylight saving it was still light, the sun just setting behind her now.

'Their property is just your side of Orange,' Matt had told her. 'Couldn't be better. Halfway between Sydney and Bangaratta. If you start out as soon as you close up shop at five-thirty, we should arrive at approximately the same time.'

Clare had been startled. She'd been expecting him to line up a hotel, or a guest-house somewhere, not a private home.

'But, Matt, who are these people? Won't they mind you bringing a perfect stranger into their home? What will I wear and what...what will be the sleeping arrangements? I thought...I mean...'

His answers to her questions had carried amusement. 'Barry Weston is an old friend of my family. A solicitor. He's mad about horse-racing and breeds his own horses. Bought this farm a few years ago and pours all his money into brood mares. He spends most weekends there. Jill, his wife, is a darling girl. A lot younger than Barry but no teenybopper. You'll like her.'

Oh, yes? she'd thought wryly.

'They've been at me to join them for a weekend for ages. They won't mind if I bring a girlfriend. In fact, they'll be delighted. And wear whatever you like. Barry and Jill hate being formal. As far as the sleeping arrangements are concerned, we'll have conveniently adjoining rooms. No need to telegraph everything, is there?'

Clare gulped as she thought of what lay ahead. And she didn't mean the road.

Accelerating along a straight stretch of highway, she almost missed the first turn-off. Thank God the sun was behind her or she probably would have!

The scenery changed somewhat with the turn. More undulating, with good grazing grass and only the occasional outcrop of huge rocks. It was top horse and sheep country, a lot of wealthy Sydney businessmen having bought properties in the area. Pitt Street farmers, they had once been called.

An hour later, Clare spotted the road Matt had told her to watch for. She swung her car into it and began counting mailboxes. The third one along on the right, he had said. There it was, a wide gateway with a sign announcing 'THREE HILLS'. The driveway behind it was very impressive, lined with white railing fences which she knew cost a fortune to build and upkeep. The sleek-coated horses grazing peacefully behind the fences looked like they'd cost a fortune too.

Clare sighed, opened the gate, drove through, then closed the gate afterwards. One didn't leave gates open in the country.

It soon became apparent why the place was called Three Hills. The road meandered over one small hill, then a second larger one, then finally snaked up the highest, upon which was perched an enormous sprawl of a house. White, two-storeyed and Spanish in flavour, it must have cost a mint.

Clare tried to still the butterflies in her stomach as she pulled up at the foot of the front steps. She was excited yet apprehensive at the same time. While she was madly—stupidly—longing to see Matt again, she wasn't looking forward to spending the weekend in a strange house with strange people.

It wasn't their being rich that bothered Clare. She had long ago determined not to let wealth and position impress or intimidate her. But she was wary about meeting Matt's friends. Would they like her? And, more importantly, would she like them? Or would she find them as plastic as she feared they might be? Lawyers occupied a box in her mind along with politicians and actors.

Clare glanced nervously around. Her car was the only one in sight, though there were several closed garages, and no one was rushing to meet her. A dog was barking somewhere. Matt had probably not yet arrived. But where were her host and hostess? Hadn't they seen her coming up the long drive? Didn't they hear the dog?

'Oh, well.' She sighed aloud and levered herself out. She was just pulling her overnight case from the boot when Matt came tripping down the steps. 'I thought I heard your car,' he said, smiling down at her. 'Here... Let me.' He took the case out of her hands. 'Jill's just popped into the shower and Barry's getting the martinis ready.' He beamed down at her. 'God, but it's good to see you.'

For some crazy unaccountable reason Clare could not find her voice. She just stood there, staring up into those beautiful blue eyes, desperately trying to think of a sophisticated thing to say.

'Damn and blast!' He dropped the case, swept her into his arms and kissed her. It was a deep hungry kiss which told her how much he still wanted her, and how much she was very definitely wanting him. She was disappointed when he stopped to just hold her.

'Darling,' he whispered into her hair afterwards, and she didn't correct him.

'Aren't you going to say anything?' he asked, pulling back to hold her at arm's length.

She smiled weakly. 'I didn't see your car,' she said.

He threw up his hands in mock exasperation. 'Is that all you have to say? I was hoping for a little more than that.' He picked up her case, took her elbow and directed her up the steps.

'Such as?'

'Such as… I missed you, Matt. I adore you, Matt. I want you to make mad, passionate love to me all weekend.'

Clare almost panicked. As usual he was going way too fast for her. He was like a runaway steamroller and she knew she had no hope of controlling him.

She was saved from answering by the front door opening and a short thick-set man coming out to stand on the porch. He just stood there, smiling expansively down at both of them. Despite the grey hair and portliness, he had an attractive face, the most engaging dimples and honest eyes. Clare liked him on sight.

'So this is Clare… I'm Barry. Drinks are ready and Jill isn't.' Barry gave her another assessing glance before turning to his friend. 'Hmm… Perhaps I should have bought my property around Bangaratta,' he said.

Clare knew her tall, slender figure looked good in the warm peach jumpsuit, her hair up in a loosely feminine style, the image she presented being one of subtle sexiness.

'For my eyes only,' Matt quipped, curling a possessive arm around her shoulders. 'You, Barry, are reduced to the position of waiter only. Lead on to the liquid refreshment.'

The house was as impressive inside as it was out. Matt led her through the front doors, across a spacious foyer and into a massive open living-room. The Spanish style continued inside with archways, tiles, rugs and heavy furniture. Barry immediately positioned himself behind the solid, wood-carved bar and began rattling a silver shaker. 'I make a mean martini, Clare.'

Matt put her case down. 'I was just thinking, Barry. Perhaps Clare would like to freshen up after her long drive?'

'Yes...yes, I would,' she said quickly, aware that she did feel sticky and uncomfortable, and far too aware of Matt. She couldn't stop looking at him, so gorgeous in tight blue jeans and blue polo shirt that seemed to make his eyes bluer. His dark brown hair was still damp and slicked straight back from his face, indicating that he wasn't long out of a shower.

'I can see you just want to get her alone, you randy devil,' Barry teased. 'Not that I blame you. First room on the left and right next to yours,' her host informed with a wicked wink.

'He's not far wrong there,' Matt whispered as he accompanied her up the stairs. His low husky words set her nerves ajangle and she stiffened, her involuntary action catching his attention. For a moment they stared at each other, and suddenly she wished that he *would* race her into the bedroom, strip off her clothes and just do it. Otherwise, thinking about it, worrying and wrangling about it, would hang over her this evening like the sword of Damocles.

He left her at the door, however, suggesting calmly that she join them in a short while. Now that the awkward moment had passed, Clare felt intense relief. It was all very well to be swept along by the romantic fantasy of the situation. A dream house. A dream man. A dream weekend. But weekends came to an end. And life went ruthlessly on...

Her room was a delight. Spacious, elegant, decorated in white and gold, with an en-suite all of its own and a small balcony which looked out over the back of the property. Rolling hills stretched to the horizon and the last rays of golden sunlight slanted right into the room and on to the queen-sized bed. A bed for two, she fancied with a quiver of her stomach.

Clare had a brief wash, tidied her hair and touched up her make-up. She wondered briefly what Barry's wife would be like. A Barbie doll of a wife or a real person, genuinely in love with her husband?

Clare doubted the latter. Younger women who married rich older men were nothing better than prostitutes in her eyes, exchanging sexual favours for the goodies money could buy. What always amazed her was why such apparently intelligent, experienced men could deceive themselves that a twenty-year-old would love them for themselves. Of course, she added with a frown, Barry was a singularly attractive older man.

With a degree of reservation, Clare left the room and was about to move down the stairs when she heard hurried footsteps behind her. She turned and her eyes opened wide.

'You must be Clare,' a wildly attractive vision in red and white announced. Red satin tights protruded from underneath the flamboyant top, on top of which rested at least a dozen gold chains. 'I'm Jill!' Bright orange-gold hair, scooped up in a messy ponytail, made her look much younger than her possible thirty years. 'So you're the lady chemist who has Matt in a bind. Hmm... His taste is on the improve.' She leant forward and kissed an astonished Clare on the cheek.

Jill slid an arm quite naturally round Clare's waist and chattered happily away as they walked down the steps and into the living area together. It was impossible not to be enchanted by her.

'About time,' Barry complained. 'We were going to call out the cavalry.'

Matt gestured for Clare to sit next to him on the brown leather lounge. She did so, feeling awkward at first, though relaxing when he curled an arm around her shoulders and pulled her close.

'You look a bit tired, Matt, love,' Jill said as she handed them both martinis.

'Nose to the grindstone, old man?' Barry asked from the bar.

'I'll say.' Matt downed half his drink. 'Now don't forget my golden rule, folks. No talking shop. And no talking damned politics! I get enough of that at home.'

'No talking religion either!' Barry declared, plopping an olive into his drink.

'How about sex?' Jill asked brightly, sending Clare's heart into a seizure.

'Sex is definitely out!' Matt tossed off with the rest of the drink.

'OK, then…' Barry sauntered over to sit down with them, bringing his glass and the cocktail shaker with him. 'What shall we talk about?'

Clare's system started working again once she realised they'd only been deciding on a conversation topic and not the night's activity. For a second then she'd thought she'd been brought to an orgy!

'How about relatives?' she suggested.

'Relatives?' they all echoed in amazement.

'I mean family trees. You can all tell me where your family comes from and so forth.'

'Splendid idea,' Matt agreed. 'And speaking of relatives, what did you two think of Tilly's intended the other week?'

'He can put his slippers under my bed any night he likes,' Jill pronounced blithely.

Barry grimaced. 'Talk about judging a book by its cover!'

'Who's Tilly?' Clare asked.

Matt leant wonderfully close. 'She's the sister I told you about. Her real name is Clothilde but Tilly suits her better. Scatty as they come but a real sweetie underneath. Still, my parents will be glad to see her settled. Her choice of men-friends hasn't always been the best. They seem to like this one, but I gather you don't think much of him, Barry?'

Barry shrugged. 'He's all right, I guess, if you like the backstabbing type. He's already walked over a few bodies in the law firm he works for, and now he's got his eyes on politics. They say the Libs have a safe seat all lined up for him for the next election. It worries me a bit that he might see Tilly more as a weapon than a wife.'

'I thought you said you weren't going to talk politics,' Jill complained.

Clare had only been half listening, her mind more involved with the way Matt's thigh was pressing firmly against hers.

'We're not talking about politics,' Matt said. 'We're talking about David McAuliffe.'

Clare almost spilt her drink, her head whipping round at the saying of that dreaded name.

'What?' Matt asked her as she stared at him, face pale, eyes blinking wide. 'What is it? Do you know David McAuliffe?'

'I...I...'

'God,' he swore. 'He's the one, isn't he? David McAuliffe. Hell, Clare, you said he was a bloody actor, not a lawyer!'

'He...he *was* an actor when I first met him,' she explained weakly. 'He was the star of the University Revue. And he stayed on in amateur theatre for a while after he graduated.'

'David McAuliffe,' Matt repeated. 'Damn and blast.'

Clare's thoughts and feelings echoed Matt's frustration.

'Would someone like to fill me in here?' Jill wailed.

'Shut up, honey,' Barry said softly. 'Look, I think Matt and Clare might like a few moments on their own. Am I right, Matt?'

'What? Oh, yes, thanks.'

Barry shepherded his mildly protesting wife from the room, leaving behind a silence that was awful. Clare could hardly think. How could fate be so cruel?

Still, this amazing revelation showed her how much she'd been deluding herself regarding her relationship with Matt. During the drive over here she'd been pretending she would settle for an affair, a romantic weekend here and there. Now she saw that underneath, she'd been hoping their relationship would develop into a full-blown love-match ending in marriage and baby bootees and happily ever after.

There was no chance of any happily ever afters now, not with David as Matt's brother-in-law, not with his ghost hanging over everything. There again, maybe there never had been any real chance for her with Matt. Maybe she was crying over a lost dream, an illusion.

And she *was* crying. Somehow, the tears had formed without her knowing and they were even now running silently down her face.

'You're still in love with him, aren't you?' Matt accused grimly.

She shook her head, unable to speak.

'Oh, yes, Clare. Very much yes. You should see your face. No words can ever deny what you still feel for that man.'

All she could do was keep on shaking her head, her eyes lowered, tears dripping off the end of her nose.

Matt sighed and stood up. 'I'll get you some tissues.'

The sound of that sigh had her eyes snapping up. 'I don't still love him,' she insisted. 'I *hate* him.'

Matt's expression told it all. He didn't believe her. 'Sure you do, honey. Sure you do. I'll get the tissues.'

He returned with half a dozen. She blew her nose and pulled herself together.

'Do you want to talk about it?' he asked after one last shudder rippled through her.

'There's nothing much to talk about. We met during my last year at university. I fell in love with him. I moved in with him. We broke up. End of story.'

'How long did you live with him?'

'Four years.'

'Four *years*! My God…'

Clare could appreciate Matt's shock. It was a long time. Longer than some marriages these days. Which was why she'd been so devastated when David had walked in one night and told her out of the blue that it was over between them.

'Why did you break up?'

She looked over at Matt. Should she tell him the unvarnished truth? Should she paint David even blacker than Barry had been painting him? If she did, what difference would it make? Matt's sister wouldn't listen to anyone. No doubt the girl was as blindly in love with David as *she* had been. Besides, David would merely deny everything she said, or twist everything around to make her sound like the typical woman scorned. She didn't doubt the daughter of a senator would make a perfect wife for him. They would probably be very happy together.

'David decided he didn't love me any more,' she said simply.

'That's it?'

'Yes.'

'Was he being unfaithful?'

'Not that I know of, but I suppose he might have been.'

Matt frowned at her. 'You sound so calm, yet a few minutes before you were crying your heart out.'

Her shrug hid a broken heart all right. But not over David.

Matt's face was darkening with frustration. 'Who would have believed it?' he finally burst out, jumping to his feet and pacing the room. 'I've never wanted a woman as much as I want you, but you're still pining after some old flame. My sister's fiancé no less! Tell me, Clare,' he said, spinning to an angry halt in front of her. 'Was he such a good lover that you'll never forget him?'

The anger and frustration in his voice forced her to say something. 'You've got it all wrong, Matt,' she said as convincingly as she could. 'I might not have forgotten David, but that's not because he was such a good lover. More because he was the most callously selfish individual I have ever known. I can assure you I do not love him any more!'

'Oh, yes?' he scoffed. 'You mean you wouldn't come running if he snapped his fingers?'

'No, I damned well wouldn't,' she denied, not wanting to talk about David any more, not wanting to be angry, just to be honest. 'The only man I would run to if he snapped his fingers these days…is you.'

Matt's eyes became two blue chips of ice. 'So you'll still sleep with me tonight?'

She closed her eyes. He was calling her bluff. But it wasn't a bluff. She loved the man, loved him like crazy. Oh, God… Her grey eyes flickered open—large, soulful eyes. 'If that's what you want,' she whispered raggedly.

He moved quickly to grasp her arms, to haul her up onto her feet and force her to look deep into his eyes. 'But is it what *you* want, Clare? Am I what you want? Or am I nothing but a substitute for a memory?'

Her mind was whirling now. She was tempted to tell

him she loved him but she was afraid, afraid he would hurt her as much as David had.

The anguish must have shown on her face, for suddenly his hands dropped away from her and his shoulders slumped. 'You're lying to me, Clare. And you're hiding things. I can see it in your eyes.'

Her mouth opened to deny everything, to tell him of her feelings when Barry burst back into the room.

'Matt, come quickly,' he yelled. 'Jill's cut her hand. Badly! She was doing the vegetables and the knife slipped.'

Clare watched, a little stunned as Matt took off in Barry's direction with long assured strides.

'Don't panic, Barry,' he was saying. 'She'll be fine. Get my bag out of the back of my car, will you?'

Both men disappeared, and Clare was left standing there, totally confused.

'Clare!' came Matt's shout from the direction of the kitchen. 'Get yourself out here! I need you!'

The scene in the kitchen rattled her. Matt was wrapping a tea-towel tightly around a pasty-faced Jill's hand, making very Dr Archer-like noises. It was on the tip of her tongue to tell them that this wasn't a television set. This was for real, as that accident the other week was for real, and they needed a *real* doctor!

But then Barry joined the group, carrying what looked like a real doctor's bag, and Clare's mouth slowly began to open. She gaped, her shocked look bringing a rueful expression to Matt's face.

'OK, so my secret's out. I *am* a real doctor. Now come over and play nurse for me.'

CHAPTER EIGHT

'I DON'T understand, Matt,' Clare said. 'Make me understand.'

He turned slowly from where he was pouring himself his third straight bourbon at the bar. Barry was upstairs putting Jill to bed. She was in shock, Matt had said, and he'd given her a sedative.

Clare shrank back from Matt's hard eyes. She had never seen him look at her like that. So remote. So indifferent. It shocked her.

'Why should I?' came his offhand answer. 'What difference would it make?'

'But you're a *doctor*!'

'So?'

'Well...why...why didn't you *tell* me, for starters?'

'When?' he retorted scornfully. 'When could I have told you and got a fair and reasonable response? The night of the ball, perhaps, after I made that speech about Bangaratta's needing a doctor? Later that night, in your apartment, after finding out what you thought of me? At the scene of that accident, maybe, right after you mocked me?'

Clare battled between guilt and irritation when she thought of that night. He'd had every opportunity to tell her then, surely. Maybe she *had* mocked him but she'd quickly apologised.

'You still should have told me,' she said unhappily.

'As you told me about McAuliffe, I suppose?' he taunted.

'That's different.'

'I don't see how.'

'David's the past and this is the present. Can't you see that you're wasting your life playing at being a doctor when you really *are* one?'

His smile was bitter. 'And you're wasting your life loving a man who doesn't love you back.'

'Probably,' she muttered, and he threw her a vicious glance, thinking no doubt that she meant David.

'Go home, Clare. I don't want you any more.'

She stared at him, tears of hurt and confusion welling up in her eyes.

'And don't bother to cry,' he lashed out. 'I have no patience with women's tears. Frankly, I'm sick to death of them!'

Outrage held her own at bay. 'Who the hell do you think you are?' she flung at him.

'I'm a man. A man who's been wanting to screw you. So what of it?'

She was speechless, too stunned to be hurt.

He laughed and came forward, glaring down at her over the rim of the glass as he downed it. 'And you've been wanting me to screw you,' he ground out, 'but you're too much of a bloody hypocrite to admit it.'

'You're drunk!' she exclaimed.

'I hope so. I'm going to need to be.'

'I'm not staying down here and listening to this.'

'Good, let's go upstairs and go to bed.'

'Go to hell!'

'Come with me,' he urged darkly, putting down the glass and dragging her into his arms.

His mouth tasted of malt whisky, and desperation. Clare was confounded by that desperation, more than his passion. This whole evening was so full of shocks that she had little defence left against his sudden fierce determination. His lips were on her neck now, his hands pulling the zipper down the front of her jumpsuit. She felt oddly detached from what he was doing, yet at the same time caught up in his dark desire.

She watched as though from a distance as he pushed her down on to the sofa, levered her bra upwards then sucked one of her breasts into his mouth. It didn't feel like *her* moaning softly, arching her back, offering her other breast up for his ministrations.

But it was.

She lay there, wallowing in the sensations, dazedly compliant as his right hand moved over her flat stomach, then slid under the elastic of her panties to search and find the heart and heat of her own desire. She groaned and arched some more.

More, more, more.

She began trembling beneath his caresses, twisting, tightening, only seconds away from release.

Barry's coming downstairs at that point put paid to any more. Fortunately he couldn't see them on the sofa when he first came into the room, giving Matt enough precious seconds to reef her bra back into place and zip up the zipper so that at least she was physically decent by the time Barry moved behind the bar and saw them.

But Clare felt anything but decent at that moment, though Barry didn't seem capable of realising what they'd been doing. Or caring, for that matter.

'She's gone to sleep,' he said blankly, spilling some brandy on to the counter as he poured half a glassful.

'God, Matt, that scared the hell out of me. If I lost Jill, I don't know what I'd do. Thank heaven you were here.'

'She wasn't in any real danger,' Matt said, standing up and walking over to sit on one of the bar-stools.

How could he seem so cool, Clare thought, when I'm still a quivering mess?

'But there was so much blood!' Barry exclaimed, shuddering.

'Some people bleed a lot.'

'Still…'

'You're in shock too, Barry. Do you want me to give you something so that you can get a good night's sleep?'

'But what about dinner?' he protested. 'You haven't had any dinner…'

'We can look after ourselves, can't we, Clare?'

Clare glared at him, but didn't have the heart to say anything that might upset Barry. He looked very shaken, the poor man.

'You go to bed, Barry,' she insisted. 'We'll be fine.'

'Come on, Bazza. No more alcohol for you if I'm to give you a shot of something.' And he took the glass out of his friend's hands.

Clare escaped to the kitchen while Matt was upstairs. She finished cutting up the stir-fry Jill was obviously preparing, more for something to do than any need to eat. Matt was gone longer than she expected so that the meal was actually sizzling in the frying pan when he returned.

'That smells good,' he said, for all the world sounding as if nothing had happened between them earlier.

She stared at him and he looked a little guilty.

'OK, so I've sobered up and I'm sorry. I overstepped

the mark and said some rotten things. But damn it all, Clare, I had provocation.'

'Like what?' she said coldly. Amazing how more in control she felt now that some time had passed, and the effect of his wild lovemaking had receded.

'Like finding out David McAuliffe was the love of your life,' he returned just as coldly. 'Like having you look at me as if I were some sort of lower order of life simply because I do what I do, and not what you *think* I should be doing.'

'A doctor takes an oath to save life,' she protested, shaking her head as she once again tried to come to terms with Matt's secret profession. How could a man choose to be an actor instead of a healer? The world was crying out for doctors, whereas it needed another useless damned actor like a hole in the head!

'Bangaratta would give its eye-teeth to have a doctor of your obvious skill,' she said with accusing eyes.

'I wouldn't be happy there.'

'Well, tough! Do you think I'm happy there either?'

'No, I don't think you are. And I think you should leave.'

She threw up her hands. 'Just like that! Leave! My God, that's rich, and so typical! There I was, thinking you were different, thinking you weren't as self-centred and selfish as…as…'

'As your dear darling David,' he finished for her. Drily. Harshly. 'Look, let's not get into this just now. It'll only spoil things even more than they're already spoilt. Let's just eat our dinner then go to bed.'

A shocked disbelief crashed through her. 'Do you honestly think I'm going to bed with you after this?'

'Yes.'

She glared at him and he glared right back.

'We're past the point of no return, Clare,' he went on bluntly. 'I know it and you know it.'

She opened her mouth to make some savage comment but then closed it again. He was right. Damn him.

But she didn't have to like it.

Her chin lifted and her grey eyes glittered angrily.

He smiled at her and she wanted to kill him.

And kiss him.

And kill him.

'You're a bastard,' she hissed through clenched teeth.

His smile turned rueful. 'I'm fast becoming one around you. Which should be to my advantage. You seem to go for bastards.'

He turned away from her pained eyes, picking up a fork and tasting the food. 'This is good, Clare. You're a talented girl, aren't you? You'll make some man a good wife one of these days.'

'But not you,' she said, and it was half a statement, half a question.

His snort was derisive. 'I can't see us ever getting married, can you? Now I suggest we both shut up, Clare, before we have another fight and you try to flounce out of here. For if you do that, I swear to you, you won't get far. I don't want to get rough with you. I really don't. But I will if I have to.'

Her eyes widened.

'It wouldn't be rape either,' he growled. 'Don't go kidding yourself, sweetheart. Anger turns you on. I turn you on. Now let's eat before I decide to skip the meal and go straight to dessert.'

* * *

They didn't turn the lights on in her bedroom. They didn't speak.

Matt turned her to him as soon as he shut the door and kissed her, holding her mouth and mind in thrall while he unzipped the jumpsuit and peeled it back off her shoulders, pushing it down off her arms till it pooled on to the floor. Lifting her out of the puddle of material, he carried her towards the bed, holding her against him with one arm while he flung back the bedclothes before placing her down on the cool white sheets.

She lay there, her eyes gradually becoming accustomed to the darkness, just enough light filtering in from the moonlit sky for her to make out his form as he undressed. He quickly stripped his shirt over his head, throwing it over the back of the chair while he kicked off his shoes and unbuttoned his jeans.

His body was as gorgeous as the rest of him, she saw, wide shoulders tapering down to slim hips and long, muscular legs. His arms and upper body looked as if he'd been doing weights, despite his saying he didn't go to the gym. There was a smattering of curls on his chest which arrowed down past his flat stomach to where he was at that moment dragging off his underpants, his jeans already gone.

Her gaze skittered away from his nakedness, unnerved by the way it made her feel. So greedy for him inside her. So…hot…

She tried watching his face when he sat down to take off his socks, keeping them steadfastly there when he bent to pick up his jeans again and remove several small plastic packets from one of the pockets. She stared at them in his hand when he walked over, still staring when he tipped them on the bedside table.

There were four.

Her eyes snapped upwards.

'I told you I'd be prepared the next time,' he said. 'Now let's get you naked…'

Getting her naked was to take quite some time, Matt being waylaid for several minutes after he removed her bra.

'You have great nipples,' he muttered later against one of them before sending his tongue forth to drive her even crazier than she already was. Suddenly, she could no longer lie passively beneath him. She had to touch him back, see for herself if he felt as good as he looked. Her left hand lifted to meet his hip before sliding down and around to encounter the object of her desire. Her fingers brushed, stroked, enclosed, squeezed, and it sent him crashing back on to the bed, gasping. She rose up on one elbow, leaning over to send her own tongue to lick at *his* nipples while she continued her merciless yet compulsive caressing.

Large fingers abruptly gripped her wrist, lifting her hand away from him. Glazed grey eyes found tortured blue ones.

'Time to use one of these,' he groaned, and reached over to pick up one of the packets. 'You put it on. I'm not capable.'

'Me?'

'Yes, you.'

Her hands trembled at first but she managed, and in truth found it an oddly erotic experience, having to keep her head and hands steady while she stroked the silky sheath down over him. She especially loved the sound of his sucked-in breath when she put her lips to him at the finish, when she let him feel the heat of her mouth for several seconds before lifting her head and looking down into his heavy-lidded eyes.

'More?' she asked with seductive softness.

He couldn't seem to speak.

She gave him more. Oh, she gave him so much more. She gave him her body and her love and her heart, and if, at the moment when they both cried out in perfect unison, her climax proving to be as cataclysmic an experience as she'd known it would be, Clare allowed herself to believe that he loved her back...then so what? This was *her* dream, wasn't it? *Her* fantasy. She could say and do and believe whatever she liked.

Clare woke to Matt kissing her softly on the lips.

For a long moment, all she remembered was the physical perfection of the night before. But then more memories washed in and she frowned.

'Matt,' she said between kisses.

'Mmm.'

'*Why* aren't you practising as a doctor?'

With a weary sigh, he rolled from her, swinging his feet over the side of the bed. 'Can't you let it go, Clare? I'm an actor now, and a damned good one. I make people happy which is as important as making them healthy.'

'Yes, but...'

He rounded on her. 'Just because we spent the night together, it doesn't give you the right to give me the third degree on what I've chosen to do with my life. I didn't *like* being a doctor. OK? And I *like* being an actor. I'm sorry you find me such a huge disappointment.'

'But I don't! I'm sorry if I...'

'For pity's sake don't apologise,' he snapped. 'I don't

want your apologies. I don't want anything from you, Clare, except what you gave me last night. If you don't think you can cope with that kind of relationship with me then you know what you can do.'

She blinked her shock up at him.

'I can't offer you any more,' he went on harshly. 'Take it or leave it.' He didn't wait for an answer, just swept up his clothes and stormed from the room.

After she showered and dressed Clare knocked on the door of his room but there was no answer. Downstairs, she found Barry in the kitchen, preparing a breakfast tray for Jill.

'How is she this morning?' Clare asked.

'Fine. Still a bit dopey from the injection Matt gave her. By the way, Matt's gone out riding.'

'Oh...'

'Did you two have an argument or something?'

'Er...sort of.'

'About Matt not telling you he was a doctor, or about McAuliffe?'

'About his not practising medicine, actually.'

'Aah...'

'Why doesn't he like being a doctor, Barry?'

Barry sighed. 'I'm afraid I can't tell you that. Both Jill and I promised him we would never discuss that with anyone. You'll have to ask him yourself.'

'I did.'

'And?'

'He wouldn't tell me.'

Barry nodded. 'Be patient, Clare. But don't press. If you love him, accept him for what he is. You do love him, don't you?'

Clare nodded, a large lump of emotion in her chest.

'I thought as much, but I wouldn't tell him just yet. As I said…be patient. Matt's a very complex man. And not inclined to be overly forthcoming about himself.'

'So I've found out,' she said bleakly.

'Can you ride, Clare?'

'Sort of.' Sam was the only horse expert in the Pride family.

'After I've taken Jill this tray, I'll take you out to the stables, saddle you a gentle horse, and point you in the direction Matt rode off in.'

'Would you?' she said eagerly.

Barry smiled. 'You do love him a lot, don't you?'

Clare was back to nodding.

She found him sitting on a riverbank, looking wretched. Her heart went out to him and she knew she could never bring herself to be the one who broke things off between them. He might only want her for sex at this point in time, but it would have to do. Who knew? Maybe Barry was right. If she was patient, things might work out in the end.

'If you've come to haul me over the coals again, don't bother,' he snarled at her as she sat down next to him. 'I'm not in the mood for lectures.'

'What *are* you in the mood for, then?' she returned, keeping her voice light.

His sidewards glance was withering. 'Don't make promises you won't keep, Clare.'

'I won't.'

He arched a sardonic eyebrow at her. 'Then am I to take it you're in agreeance with the arrangement I offered you?'

'Yes.'

Oddly enough, he looked furious. 'Just like that! A

simple yes, after all the reasons you gave me why you wouldn't enter into such a relationship.'

Her heart was starting to thud, both with her own recklessness, and what she was seeing in that suddenly smouldering gaze. Desire, as hot and harsh as a desert wind.

'I...I've changed my mind,' she said shakily. 'It's a woman's privilege to change her mind, isn't it?'

Those blazing blue eyes hardened, then narrowed. Without hesitation, he twisted to take her shoulders and push her back into the sweet-smelling grass, his head bending to nuzzle at the base of her throat. 'Have you come prepared, then?' he muttered against the throbbing pulse he found there.

Clare gasped her shock, and her excitement. Surely he didn't mean to make love to her *here*!

'I see you haven't,' he growled, his head lifting when his hands moved down to unsnap the waistband of her jeans. She was stunned by the look of ruthless determination in his eyes. Stunned, yet at the same time incredibly aroused.

'No worries,' he ground out. 'I'm sure I can find plenty of ways around that little hurdle.'

Which he did.

Madly. Mercilessly. Marvellously.

CHAPTER NINE

'MUM knows, you know,' Samantha said cockily, perching herself up on a kitchen stool.

'Knows what?'' Clare continued peeling the potatoes. It was the Tuesday after her trip to Three Hills and she was baby-sitting her kid sister while her parents went to a bridge party.

'That you're having an affair with some old boyfriend from Sydney.'

'Is that so?' she said.

'Uh-huh.' Sam grinned, clearly enjoying the topic of conversation. 'Everyone in Bangaratta knows about the phone calls and the flowers, and they're all wondering where you went last weekend. Mum says you must have spent it with the flower-sender and that you're sleeping with him.'

'Mum said that to *you*?' Clare was shocked.

'Oh, of course not! I overheard her saying so to Dad. She also said that you were a damned fool. Something about why should a man buy a cow if someone's giving him milk for free?'

Clare clamped her mouth tightly shut. If she opened it at that moment, she would definitely say something she'd regret.

'But I don't agree with Mum,' Sam rattled on. 'I reckon if you fancy a guy then why not sleep with him. No one expects to marry a virgin these days.'

'Sam! For goodness' sake, you're only a child! This is not the013'

'Are you in love with him?' Sam broke in.

Clare swallowed, images flooding her mind, none of them loving. It worried her, the way Matt took perverse satisfaction in reducing her to begging, or in making her make him beg. It also bothered her that by the end of the weekend at Three Hills she didn't seem to care any more that their relationship was only sexual. All she sought from him was his body in hers and the mindless pleasure they gave to each other. Matt was succeeding in making a travesty of what they could have shared together, and suddenly she hated him for it.

'Sis? You haven't answered me. Are you in love with him?'

'There is no him,' she bit out. 'I just needed to get away for a while. And you can tell dear Mum that I'll be getting away more often in future!'

Later that evening, when it was time to watch *Bush Doctor*, Clare astounded Sam by refusing to turn it on, saying there was a current affairs programme she preferred on Channel Two.

'But I wanted to watch Matt,' Sam whined.

'You told me you didn't like that show much,' Clare argued. 'And that Matt was too old to be interesting.'

'That was before I met him. I think he's yummy now. Oh, please, Clare, please, please, pretty please.'

Clare gave in, and had never spent a more miserable hour in her entire life. She wanted to cry, to throw something at the television, to shatter that hatefully handsome face. Instead, she sat and cried inside, knowing that when he snapped his fingers she would run to him, knowing that she had made the same stupid mistake again. Fallen in love with the wrong man.

Naturally, he'd sent her off home on Sunday evening, saying he would call. And naturally, she was living for the moment when he did. But he hadn't called as yet, which was why watching him on television that night was sheer torture.

He didn't call on the Wednesday either, or the Thursday. By Friday Clare was frantic that Matt would never call again, so that when he did call the shop that morning—saying curtly that he couldn't stop and chat but if she agreed to come there would be a pre-paid first-class return ticket waiting for her at Dubbo airport for the Saturday afternoon flight to Sydney, and that he'd be waiting for her at the luggage carousel—she meekly agreed. After he'd hung up she stared down into the dead receiver before dropping it back into its cradle with numb fingers then slumping down at her bench and burying her head in her hands.

Dear God, whatever was going to become of her?

A gentle hand on her shoulder made her jump. 'That same man again, Clare?' Sally asked, not unkindly.

Clare nodded.

'Maybe you should go to Sydney and see him,' she said. 'Handsome and rich might not make for a perfect life-partner, but no one's perfect, Clare. If you wait to find perfect, you'll be a lonely old lady till the day you die.'

Clare looked up. 'Why, Sally…that was quite profound.'

Sally frowned. 'What does "profound" mean?'

'It means smart. Real smart.'

Sally looked pleased.

'I think I will do what you suggested, but if I do, I might be a little late opening the shop on Monday morning. How about you have a sleep-in and don't arrive here till ten?'

'Sounds good to me!'

'Oh, and Sally…'

'Yes?'

'Try not to tell anyone the reason, will you?'

Sally looked most put out for second, but then she grinned. 'I can keep a secret if you can.'

'Oh? What's your secret?'

'I'm going to have a baby!'

It was muggy and overcast when Clare left Bangaratta the following afternoon to drive to Dubbo. By the time the flight landed at Mascot it had started to rain, and she'd begun to worry that Matt might not be there to meet her where he said he'd be.

But he was, his gorgeous body encased in casual bone-coloured trousers and a brightly patterned shirt in blues and browns, those wraparound opaque sunglasses doing their best to hide his identity. Her own jeans and black T-shirt seemed plain by comparison, though she'd gone to quite a bit of trouble with her hair and face.

Seeing him standing there, looking so sexy but rather remote, brought instant butterflies to her stomach. Clare had spent most of the flight down, secretly hoping that their reunion would be like something out of the movies. They would look at each across the crowded room, run into each other's arms and openly declare their love for each other. Any such stupidly romantic hope flew out of the window when Matt walked coolly up to her, took her lightly by the shoulders and gave her a peck on the cheek.

'I'm glad you decided to come, Clare,' he said. 'I've missed you. Have you missed me?'

'Yes,' was all she could manage. He was wearing some kind of tangy aftershave which made her very conscious of him. Dazedly, she wondered if her own perfume was doing the same incredible things to him.

'Thanks for sending me the ticket,' she said thickly.

'My pleasure.'

'You're...you're being awfully polite.'

'Better than my ripping off your clothes and throwing you on the carousel,' he drawled. 'Which is what I'd like to do at this moment.'

Clare felt a wave of heat flush her skin.

'Which is your suitcase?' he asked abruptly. 'I think the sooner we get out of here, the better.'

'That one,' she pointed out tautly, nervous of Matt's brittle mood, yet stirred by the sexuality simmering beneath it.

'Right,' he muttered, and reached over to grab it.

Once outside the terminal, they had to stop at the kerb, a sudden downpour halting any further progress.

'Let's run for it,' he suggested after a few seconds' fraught silence.

They did, and got sopping wet in the process.

'I'm soaked through!' she exclaimed as she was bundled into the passenger seat of his very sleek silver-grey sedan.

'That's all right.' He leant over her to snap her seat-belt into place. 'I like you wet.'

She stared up at him, knowing where his eyes were looking behind the sunglasses. Her breathing was coming thick and fast and she could feel her nipples straining against the thin damp T-shirt. He hesitated, then his mouth covered hers, his tongue taking its time before sliding between her gasping lips and giving her a dress rehearsal of the real thing.

As usual, he had more control than she did, pulling away and smiling wryly as he slammed the car door and walked round to climb in behind the wheel.

'Where are you taking me?' Clare asked once they were under way.

'Somewhere private.'

'Your unit in Kirribilli?'

'Uh-huh.'

It wasn't long before they were into the city and on the approaches to the harbour bridge. Two years it had been since Clare had seen the sights of Sydney and even with the light drizzle, it was still as breathtakingly beautiful as ever. More beautiful in a way, with the streets shimmering after the rain, the city's lights reflecting in the wet surfaces. She peered down from the bridge at the harbour below and marvelled anew. A magnificent city in a magnificent setting.

She felt stirred by its beauty and its throbbing life. It excited her as much as the man beside her did. She flicked a sidewards glance at Matt. He'd said she wasn't happy living in Bangaratta and he'd been right.

Matt swung the car down off the Cahill Expressway into a series of steep narrow streets which led into a cul-de-sac at the bottom of which rose a tall block of home units. After parking the car in a security-guarded underground car park they took an elevator in silence up to the twentieth floor, the ride excruciatingly tense for Clare. She didn't like being treated as a sex object, yet she couldn't find the words to object. She loved Matt too much, and wanted him too much.

The doors whirred back. Matt picked up her suitcase, and shepherded her out on to a richly flowered carpet. With her suitcase in one hand and the other at her elbow, he guided Clare along the hallway and stopped in front of a cream-painted door marked number six. He produced a gold key from his set of keys and slipped it into the brass lock, turning and pushing the door open in one fluid movement.

The apartment was not at all as Clare had imagined, except for its spectacular view of the harbour from the balcony. She had rather pictured an austerely furnished place, all stark and functional to go with Matt's busy lifestyle. Instead it was warm and friendly-looking, with soft earth colours and masses of pot-plants.

'Goodness, Matt,' she said, pleased to break the electric atmosphere. 'You must have a secret passion for gardening. All these ferns and plants!'

'They came with the place,' he said nonchalantly, walking over to open one of the doors that came off the L-shaped lounge and dining area. 'My bedroom,' he said, and placed her suitcase inside. 'It has its own en-suite but there is another bathroom.' He gestured to a second door, then turned to slide back another. 'Kitchen in here, and that last door over behind you is a second bedroom. We won't be needing that,' he added firmly.

'Perhaps I'll have a shower and change,' she said, trying to sound natural. 'Are we going out to dinner?'

He walked over to her and pulled her in his arms. 'Don't be ridiculous. Now that I have you here, I'm not going anywhere but to bed.'

Clare's handbag slipped from her fingers on to the

gold carpet and she slid her arms up around his neck. Their kiss was savage and frantic and desperate, echoing their intense need for each other. Matt's hands slid down her back to grab large handfuls of her buttocks as he ground her hard against him.

'God, Matt,' she protested when his mouth finally moved from hers down to her neck.

He abandoned her with a ragged sigh. 'Sorry,' he muttered, and wrenched his sunglasses off to reveal smouldering eyes. 'Our week apart has had a most unfortunate effect on me. But you're right. I'd really much rather not hurry this. Go and take your shower. I'll do likewise.'

She agreed, though not without a moment of perverse rebellion. I want you now...*now*, her body was crying out.

The shower cooled her blood a little. But only a little. Not wanting to look at herself naked in the mirror, she hurriedly dragged on the ivory silk robe she had brought with her before brushing her hair and dabbing some fresh perfume behind her ears and on her wrists. The bathroom was well equipped for female guests, she saw, with plenty of assorted toiletries right down to a spare toothbrush.

Such sights sent horrid thoughts tumbling into her mind. Had Matt had other women here since meeting her? He'd promised her exclusivity, but was he keeping to that? His obvious sexual frustration soothed the ghastly thoughts somewhat, but it was her own intense need for him that finally forced her to brush any lingering doubts aside. He was out there in his bedroom waiting to make love to her. She would not do or say anything that might spoil that. *Could* not. Ever!

Matt's bedroom was empty, one single lamp throwing a dim light across the large bed whose doona was already pulled back in readiness. She could hear the sound of the shower still running in the en-suite and hesitated about actually climbing into the bed to await Matt's arrival. She felt too excited to lie still. Finally she moved over to the large window and drew back the heavy gold curtains.

The view was unimpaired by rooftops, for they were so high up. Rain-clouds covered the stars but the moon was managing to find a passage, a pale version of its usual brilliance against the grey sky. Clare became transfixed, watching its trek in and out of the clouds—a ghostly ship drifting in a treacherous sea mist.

She jumped slightly when Matt's hands closed gently over her shoulders.

'Sorry about the lack of stars,' he murmured, pulling her back against him so that his lips nuzzled one ear. She shivered, goose-bumps springing up all over her flesh. 'Cold?' he asked, rubbing her arms.

'No…' She closed her eyes, turned her head slightly away from the tantalising tongue and tried to relax against him. He continued to caress her arms, his mouth moving to cover her ear fully so that she was hotly aware of his rapid breathing. Her own heart was hammering wildly and tremors ran up and down her legs. She went to turn round, to face him, but he denied her, wrapping his arms around her waist from behind and forcing her to remain as they were. 'Slowly…slowly…' he soothed as though he were talking to a flighty horse.

His hands moved to unloop the sash around her waist, taking his time in parting the silk. Did she moan as a fingertip brushed bare flesh? Perhaps… Her eyes were definitely wide, her lips parted.

And then she saw it… A faint reflection of herself in the window, half-naked against him. She watched, dry-mouthed and heart pounding, as his slender fingers roved across her flat stomach then travelled upwards towards her small but exquisitely swollen breasts. She held her breath as they grazed lightly across the erect peaks, but then, to her consternation, his hands lay unsatisfactorily motionless around them.

'So lovely,' he murmured.

She leant back into him, needing to be closer. His hands skimmed down to curve round her hips and he undulated slowly against her, making her fiercely aware of his arousal. For the first time since he had come into the room she realised that he was totally nude. Only her silk robe stood between them. He moved against her and the moving—together, yet not together—was sheer torture. Clare could no longer stand it.

'Matt,' she rasped, whirling in his arms and seeking his mouth.

He laughed, and instead of kissing her, stripped off her robe and swept her up into his arms. 'You're an impatient little thing, aren't you?' he growled, and carried her over to the bed. He lowered her into the softness then stood over her for a moment, staring down with darkened narrowed eyes. Bending, he slid a hand around her neck, lifting her head and kissing her without letting any other part of their nakedness connect. Her mouth opened eagerly beneath him, her body growing ever more restless. Again, when she reached for him, he pulled back, watching her under half-closed lids.

'Don't tease me, Matt,' she groaned.

He smiled and lay down beside her, running his hands over her body in long stroking movements. 'I love teasing you,' he said thickly. 'I love it when you moan. I love it when you make me moan. Do it, Clare. Make me moan.' He rolled her up on to his chest and waited. She bent her head, her hair falling forward. He pushed it back and held it there, then pulled her slowly down on to his mouth.

Clare had never been all that fond of taking the assertive role in lovemaking with David. But that was because he always directed then criticised. Do this, he would say. Now do that. No, harder, no, softer, or whatever. Matt, having once indicated he wanted her to control things, just lay back and let her do as she willed, and he never ever said a critical word, the only sounds leaving his lips those of arousal or urgency or ecstasy.

He groaned deep in his throat when her tongue entered his mouth to slowly caress his, then remained tensely silent when she took her lips away to move down his body. It was only when she took one of his nipples between her teeth that he gasped. She tugged on it gently, then licked it, revelling in the sounds of his pained pleasure. His gasps turned to low tortured moans, however, when her mouth moved lower…

'Oh, dear God,' she heard him mutter once, and the heady sense of sexual power sent liquid fire along her veins.

She didn't stop till she felt every muscle in his body stiffen, till he was trembling on the brink. Only then did she reach for the protection he'd subtly left beside the bed, noting as she did that his eyes were glazed, his lips parted, his breathing fast and shallow.

'Hurry,' he groaned. 'For God's sake, hurry…'

She laughed and did no such thing, letting his passion subside a little while she sheathed his quivering flesh. When she finally consented to take him deep inside her, an animal growl punched from his lungs. He grasped her hips and tried to move her up and down, but she resisted, stretching languorously upwards then arching back, the palms of her hands flat on the bed on either side of her ankles.

Her movements were gentle at first, soft, pulsating movements, but gradually her own need took over and she began rising and falling in an impassioned rhythm, squeezing tightly around him, drawing him deeper and deeper into her heat. There came a point, however, when all thought ceased, all patience, Clare surrendering to the explosive climax that tore through them both. Her pleasure had never been sharper, her orgasm more intense. When she was finally released from its all-consuming sensations she collapsed upon him, hugging him tight and shuddering her satisfaction.

'Oh, Matt,' she cried, a disbelieving bliss in her voice.

His arms slid around her, tightening as his lips brushed the top of her head. 'Yes, I know. That's how I feel, too. It's never been like this for me before.'

Clare thrilled to his words. It was not a declaration of love but it was damned close. Barry had been so right. All she'd needed was a little patience.

'It's never been like this for me before either,' she whispered.

'Not even with McAuliffe?'

Her head snapped up off his chest. 'No, never!' she denied fiercely.

'And you're not still in love with him?'

'I haven't been in love with him for donkey's years.'

'Good. Now put your head back down, or you'll get a crink in your neck.'

'But, Matt, I...'

'Hush, my darling,' he murmured, placing three fingers against her lips. 'The last thing I want to do this weekend is spend precious time talking about some old flame of yours. Keep those lovely lips of yours for more important pastimes.'

'You're a wicked man, do you know that?'

'I am when I'm around you.'

'But we can't make love *all* weekend?'

'I do realise that. Occasionally, we'll have to get up to go to the bathroom.'

Clare laughed. 'What about food? Don't you think we might need a bit of sustenance from time to time?'

'I can live on love for twenty-four hours.'

Clare gulped. Had he realised what he'd just said?

'Then so can I,' she choked out.

For twenty-four hours they were as happy as honeymooners. And, just like honeymooners, rarely left the bedroom, though they did bring in the odd snack or two. Matt even took the phone off the hook so that they wouldn't be disturbed.

He never said the word love again, but he showed Clare in many ways that he did love her. With his tenderness. His consideration. His passion. She felt in her heart that it was only a matter of time before he told her outright. Meanwhile, she was content to go along with what Matt wanted, which seemed to begin and end with their exploration of each other on a purely physical level. Clare understood it was a perfectly natural thing at the beginning of a relationship and in truth, she was enjoying their sexual preoccupation every bit as much as Matt was.

It was on the Sunday evening that their Utopia came to an abrupt end.

They were just finishing dressing, having laughingly decided that a breath of fresh air was called for, when there came a frantic knocking at the door. Matt hurried to open it.

'Thank heaven you're here!' Bill rushed in, clearly at his wits' end. 'Why in God's name did you take the blasted phone off the hook?' Upon sighting Clare standing in the bedroom door, he looked startled. 'What the...?' He turned towards Matt, a questioning look on his face.

'Clare came down to Sydney for the weekend,' he explained evenly.

Bill flicked Matt an odd glance and Matt's face took on a closed look. 'What's the panic?' he asked.

'Your mother's been trying to contact you all afternoon. In the end she got on to me and asked me to come over here and see if you were home.'

'What's wrong?'

'It's Tilly.'

'What about Tilly?'

'She tried to kill herself. Took an overdose of sleeping tablets.'

Clare came forward. 'Oh, Matt...'

His sigh was weary. 'Where is she? In hospital?'

'No... She's at your parents' home. The doctor's been and said she didn't have to go to hospital. Apparently, she had some sort of fight with her fiancé and decided life wasn't worth living.'

'I see.'

'Your mother says Tilly insists on seeing you. She won't tell Mrs Sheffield anything. And your father's away.'

'Isn't he always?' Matt grumbled. 'OK, I'll come. What about you, Clare? You might as well come too. You have to meet the family soon enough, and why not at its worst?'

He really didn't give her the opportunity to refuse, bustling her out of the unit in a matter of seconds. The ride in the car was tense and silent, Clare concerned that she might come face to face with David.

'Don't look so stricken,' Matt reassured her. 'With a bit of luck, McAuliffe won't be there, but either way I need to know, Clare—not for my sake, but Tilly's—exactly what happened between the two of you, especially what broke you up.'

Which did seem logical, Clare reasoned, but suddenly, her whole being rebelled against telling Matt. It was so demeaning.

'Please, Clare…'

So she told him, as calmly and as dispassionately as she could. He listened without comment and asked not a single question.

The Sheffield home was situated in Lindfield, in a quiet tree-lined street. It was a gracious home, two-storeyed, with small windows and creepers over the wall, reminiscent of an English manor house. Bill had not come with them but Clare still felt awkward trailing along behind as Matt strode up the front path to knock loudly at the door.

She moved nervously from foot to foot as they waited on the porch for someone to answer. After an agonising few seconds the door was finally opened and Clare's worst fears materialised.

'What the hell are you doing here, McAuliffe!' Matt exclaimed.

CHAPTER TEN

MATT pushed David aside and strode into the entranceway. Clare, who had been in the shadows, stepped forward as well. It was only then that David saw her, his expressive brown eyes widening appreciably. '*Clare*?'

'Hello, David,' she murmured, looking away from his astounded face and moving to stand at Matt's side.

'I think the reunion chatter can wait,' Matt said curtly. 'Where's my mother?'

'Upstairs,' David replied, his eyes still on Clare. 'With your sister.'

'I repeat, McAuliffe, what in the bloody hell are you doing here?'

'He's being very patient and understanding…'

They all spun round to see a tall, gaunt-faced woman coming down the staircase.

'…and it's not like you, Matt, to be so rude.'

'Mother, I013'

'And who is this?' Mrs Sheffield asked stiffly as she came forward. Clearly, from her tone of voice, she thought it an inappropriate time for her son to bring a strange woman into her home.

'Clare is a friend of mine. We were just going out when Bill contacted me.'

'And you brought her *here…now*?'

Clare felt terrible. Mrs Sheffield was glaring at her as though she were from another planet. David kept looking her over as though he was seeing the real Clare for the first time. And Matt was not his usual cool self.

'For God's sake, Mother, I don't see why you should criticise my actions when Tilly and her...fiancé...' he tossed a disparaging hand in David's direction '...are the ones causing all the strife. What did you expect me to do? Leave Clare in the lurch? Now where is this sister of mine?'

'Come with me,' his mother murmured. 'I think your...er...friend...should stay down here. David can take her into the study for a drink.'

Matt gave both Clare and David a penetrating look, then said, 'Good idea,' abruptly before turning and going upstairs with his mother.

Somewhere a door banged shut and the house fell eerily silent. Neither of them had moved. David was still staring at Clare and for her part she wondered why she was so embarrassed and tongue-tied. She owed this man nothing—neither explanations nor excuses.

'It's been a long time, Clare,' he finally said, then added, 'And I must say the years have treated you well. You look positively...stunning.'

She glared at him and thought, But you haven't changed a bit, David. You're still the most insidiously handsome man I've ever seen. And still the biggest liar!

Her eyes travelled from his superbly groomed dark blond hair down his classical sculptured face past his sulkily sexy mouth to his elegantly clad figure. Once, his mere presence had stirred her. She knew that he could kiss her now and she would remained unmoved.

'You're looking well, too,' she said coolly, though underneath she was not altogether calm. Matt's expression had bothered her when he suggested she go with

David. Did he think she *still* harboured secret feelings for this man? She hoped not, for nothing was further from the truth.

Looking around at the many closed doors she asked, 'Where's the study? I could do with that drink.'

His mouth curved back into a sexy smile. 'So could I.'

He walked across the wide hall, threw open a door and stepped back, gesturing for Clare to go in. She did so, quickly taking in the masculine décor people favoured in studies. Padded leather chairs, dark stained shelves, a heavy wooden desk with intricately carved legs. Across one wall, under the lines of richly bound books, ran a long wide shelf on which sat a well stocked drinks tray. David crossed to it, turned over two clean glasses then lifted his velvety brown eyes. 'What will it be?'

'Don't you remember?' she asked with a touch of venom. *She* remembered every rotten damned thing about *him*.

His lips twitched in a wry grimace. 'You used to follow my lead.'

Her own expression was equally sardonic. 'So I did, but things have changed since then. Nowadays I have opinions of my own.'

'You always had opinions of your own, Clare,' he inserted softly.

'But in the end yours were the only ones that counted.'

He shrugged.

'I'll have a cognac,' she said.

He poured two of the same and handed one over. She had not sat down. They were eye to eye, David not being an overly tall man and Clare wearing heels. 'Here's to old friends,' he whispered, lifting the glass to his mouth, his eyes never leaving hers.

She drank. After the glass left her lips, a rueful little smile settled. 'We'll never be that, David.'

'Oh?' He turned and perched on the edge of the desk. 'Sit down, Clare. You make me nervous standing there.'

She gave him a cold look and sat down in the nearest chair. 'Nothing makes you nervous, David,' she said drily.

'Sarcasm, Clare?'

'The truth.'

'Aah… Such a black and white person you always were, Clare. Don't you find such views constricting?'

'I'm not such a black and white person any more, David. I've learnt—by my mistakes—that things can be grey at times.'

He sighed. 'Such a pity you didn't know that two years ago.'

'You mean I would have accepted your offer to remain on as your mistress, after you sweetly told me marriage was out?'

'Why not? I might have eventually changed my mind. After all, just look at you now. So poised, so confident, so sophisticated. And being squired around by one of the most eligible bachelors in town. A far cry from the mousy little student I first met and knew.'

Her laughter was high-pitched and hard. '*Knew*! Such a lukewarm word. It hardly does justice to our relationship.' She stood up, coming towards him with bitterness in her eyes. 'Four years, David. Four years of my life, devoted entirely to you. Four years of being a pretend wife without any of the real benefits. That was a big concession of my principles, David, but you were incredibly persuasive. I only gave in because I thought you loved me, thought you meant it when you promised we would be married as soon as you were on your feet. You lied to me, David. You lied to me and used me. You took and you took, and you gave nothing back!'

'Really? I seem to recall you got quite a bit out of me?' His smile was faintly malicious.

'Trust you to be crude! Sex was all you ever thought about.'

'And didn't you love it?' He put his drink down and slid off the desk. Then he took the glass from her hand and disposed of it likewise. 'Clare,' he murmured, turning back to stand close. 'Don't let's argue. This is all in the past. Surely we can be friends now? After all, you seem to have put aside those principles of yours again, haven't you?'

She stared up at him, not knowing what he was talking about.

'Matt Sheffield is well known for his appetite for women. Surely you don't expect me to believe you're not sleeping with him?'

'I don't think my private life is any of your business, David,' she said angrily.

His eyes held a parody of concern, and if she hadn't known him better she might have thought he still cared about her. 'I wouldn't like you to make the same mistake twice, my love.'

Her mouth went dry. 'In what way?' she croaked.

'Well, surely you aren't expecting Matt Sheffield to marry you, are you?'

'I'm not expecting anything,' she bit out.

'That's good. I'd hate to see you hurt again the way

I hurt you. You've no idea how deeply I've regretted the way things turned out, Clare.' His hand reached out to lightly touch her cheek. His smile was incredibly warm and convincing. 'Seeing you here tonight, looking so lovely, makes me think I made a stupid mistake. I should never have listened to my father.'

With a melodramatic sigh he turned away, his shoulders slumping, and Clare grudgingly admired his acting ability. There again, he'd had plenty of practice! Naturally, she was supposed to ask how his father—part of the family that she conveniently never met—had influenced the outcome of their relationship. She would have ignored David's ploy, if her curiosity hadn't got the better of her.

'What about your father?' she asked, and waited for the imaginative lies.

David swung back to face her, an apologetic look in those velvety brown eyes. 'When my father came home that last year from overseas and found out we were living together, he was furious. He assured me that if I married you I would never be offered a partnership in the law firm I was working for, nor would he personally back my political career. He pointed out that to marry you—a nobody from the bush—would greatly hinder my chances of reaching the top. He explained that to be successful one needed everything going for one—including the right wife.

'He then went on to convince me that I wasn't in love with you anyway, that it was a sexual infatuation, and that all young men go through similar infatuations. I believed him, much to my discredit. I believed him and I let you go. That's the truth and I'm sorry.'

Clare had the awful feeling that he was about to take her in his arms, so she stepped backwards and sat down.

'I was wrong,' he continued smoothly. 'Very wrong… I know that now… Say you forgive me?'

Clare was dumbfounded. Did he really think he could wave a magic wand and all would be forgiven? Did he honestly conceive that this heartfelt confession would sway her opinion of him? He was an out-and-out bastard and nothing would change that. Suddenly she remembered what had brought her to this house in the first. 'Why did Matt's sister try to kill herself?' she asked.

He shrugged and turned away, picking up his drink and draining it. 'She thought I was seeing another woman,' he said nonchalantly.

'And were you?'

'Of course not!'

'Do you love Tilly?'

His head jerked up. 'Who? Oh, you mean Clothilde. She's a sweet girl and I love her very much.'

'What if her surname had been Pride and not Sheffield?'

'Then I wouldn't have let myself fall in love with her in the first place,' he said with a wry twist. 'Even I learn by experience, Clare. And believe it or not, it hurt me to let you go.'

Clare almost choked on the spot. Let her go? The bastard had thrown her out, lock, stock and barrel! She recalled how she'd come home from work that day to find her bags packed and ready. She'd been stunned by his cold dismissal, then blown away by his last-minute magnanimous offer that she could keep the designer dress he'd bought for her to wear to the ball the following week—which of course she would never attend with him—pointing out callously that there would be more presents like that if, once she found a place of her own, she let him visit her from time to time. He'd been totally unmoved when she'd told him where to go in no uncertain terms, yet here he was claiming he'd been hurt by their 'break-up'.

She stared into those deep brown eyes and shook herself mentally. He would never learn, never change.

David gave her a searching look. 'How come you know Matt Sheffield anyway? I heard you eventually went back to Bangaratta to live.'

'I did.'

'Have you known each other long?' David persisted.

'Quite a while.'

'Why are you in Sydney? Are you thinking of moving back here?'

Clare hesitated then decided not to tell this man another thing. 'No, just visiting.'

'Where are you staying? Maybe we could go out for lunch one day?'

'I don't think so, McAuliffe,' Matt pronounced coldly as he came into the room.

David was not easily intimidated, however. 'Why not?' His face was the perfect mask of innocence. 'We're old friends.'

'That's not quite the way I heard it.'

David threw her a look as if to say she was a naïve fool to have told Matt about their past. 'I see,' he muttered. 'Well? How's Clothilde?'

'She'll be OK…with time, but she doesn't want to see you again, McAuliffe. Here's your ring.' Matt thrust it into his hand. 'Now get the hell out of here!'

'Just hold it there a moment!' David countered forcefully. 'I'm not going anywhere till I talk to Clothilde, make her understand she was mistaken.'

Matt had walked round behind the desk and was standing with his arms folded. 'Don't waste your breath. She won't believe you. The private detective hired to follow you did a good job.'

David could not quite contain the shocked gasp. 'Private detective!' Then he pulled himself together. 'You're lying. Clothilde would never do that and besides, your mother said nothing about013'

'My mother only just found out,' Matt cut in. 'Apparently my father had his suspicions and he knew just what to do. You're damned lucky he's away at the moment. As it is, I'm barely restraining myself from doing you a physical injury, so I suggest you get out while the going's good.'

'I still say this is a misunderstanding. Or a blatant pack of lies!'

'Oh, for pity's sake, surely you don't want it spelled out, do you?' His lips curled with distaste. 'I have dates, photostats of motel bookings, even photos.'

Clare's eyes were riveted on David and his expressions were a revelation. From outrage to a blasé resignation in a split-second. Now that there wasn't any point continuing the bluff, he took his exposure as a philanderer with incredible calm. Love Tilly? David only loved a woman for as long as she fitted in with his plans. Clare instantly knew that there had been other women while he'd been living with her as well. All those late late nights working back at the office… My God! What a naïve little fool she had been!

'In that case, I guess it's time to make a discreet departure. Nice seeing you again, Clare.' He made a move towards the door then stopped, turning unexpectedly vicious eyes back over his shoulder. 'I can't see why you should be acting holier than thou, Sheffield. If I know Clare, you're screwing the hell out of her, and at the same time shacking up with Tiffany Makepiece. Ah, poor Clare, I see you didn't know about your lover's live-in lover. Successful business woman. Works as PR for an international cosmetics firm. Owns a fancy unit down at Kirribilli. No doubt you'll meet her some time, since you've so much in common.'

He threw Matt a spiteful look. 'You're wondering how I knew about Miss Makepiece, dear chap? Tch, tch. I dare say your secret is not well known but sisters will talk, won't they? See you around.' He walked out, leaving a stunned silence behind.

Matt was the first to speak. 'Clare. Don't jump to conclusions. Please...'

She could not find her breath to say anything, her mind a hopeless jumble. Don't jump to conclusions, he was asking her so calmly. My God, she didn't have to jump! It was a swift savage slide to the truth.

'Clare...' Matt moved quickly to her, taking her hands in his and pulling her to her feet. 'It's not what you're thinking...'

'What am I thinking?' she said like an automaton.

'That I've been cheating on you, stringing you along while I've been living with another woman.'

'And you haven't?'

'Dear God... How can I answer that with a simple yes or no?'

'I could,' she said brokenly, 'if you asked me.'

Slowly she extricated her hands from the warmth of his clasp. She needed to think and she couldn't do that properly while he was touching her, staring down at her like that. 'Then who is this Tiffany?' she asked shakily, a type of angry despair beginning to seethe inside her. It seemed impossible that she had actually done it again; fallen for a man who was no better than a two-timing con-man.

He closed his eyes for a few seconds. 'God!' he sighed.

Clare moved away from him, reclaiming her drink from the desk and downing it with one gulp. 'I'm waiting,' she said in a low, deadly voice.

He threw up his hands in defeat. 'I don't know where to begin.'

'Strange. You're usually so good with words. Perhaps I can help by asking you a few questions? The unit where we've been staying… It belongs to this Tiffany woman?' Not that Clare needed to ask. The evidence had been there before David had said anything. Matt's reluctance to give her that particular phone-number, the feminine furnishings, the plants, the toiletries, Bill's look when he found her there. It all added up.

Matt's face showed anguish and he began to move towards her. 'Clare, you…'

'Stay right where you are!' she flung at him. 'If you come any closer, I'll walk right out of here, Matt. I mean it!'

He stopped and his whole body sagged. 'I know you do.'

'Then answer my question.'

'Before I do, let me ask you one. Do you love me?'

'Goddamn you, Matt, you have no right to013'

'*Do* you?' he cut in forcefully.

'Yes,' she bit out. 'You must know I do.'

'I hoped you did, because I certainly love you.'

Clare groaned. Oh, how she had wanted to hear him say that. But not now. Not in these circumstances.

'What kind of love do you love with me with?' he asked fiercely. 'Does it include admiration and trust and respect? I left you here tonight with McAuliffe because I loved you that way. I thought it was a good idea for you to face your past, to be sure you didn't have any traces of feeling left for that bastard. What I'm about to tell you might test your love, Clare, but it shouldn't destroy it...if it's a true love and not the kind of superficial and strictly sexual love I've always been wary of.'

She thought she was beyond feeling any more pain, but somehow his words brought more. He was like David, not giving in, not admitting anything even when caught red-handed. Matt had betrayed her, and he was going to try to rationalise it.

'You're living with this woman?' she rasped.

'I have been.'

'It's her unit, isn't it? And you've been living there with her the whole time you've been pursuing me. My God! You even rang me from her phone, didn't you? *Didn't you*?' she screamed.

He gave her a pained look. 'It's not as cut and dried as that, Clare.'

'Were you or were you not living there with her when you met me?' she demanded through clenched teeth. 'Yes or no!'

'Yes.'

'Oh, my God,' she whimpered, a bleak sickness washing through her. She leant against the desk so that she wouldn't fall.

'Clare...Clare...' He came up behind her, steadying

her with gentle hands. 'Try to understand. That first time, I didn't expect to meet someone like you out at Bangaratta. Tiffany had been overseas on business for weeks. I was madly attracted to you. I hadn't made love for a long time. What happened between us just happened. Even you can't be so unfair as to say that incident was all my fault.'

Clare wrenched away. 'Of course not!' she spat at him. 'You fell into the clutches of a right little raver. Why, I almost raped you, didn't I?'

'Don't try to belittle what happened, Clare. We both know now that something happened between us that night other than just sex. But the next day…you were so adamant you wanted nothing to do with me, then on the flight home Bill made some comment about how I was crazy to get involved with someone who would want so much more than I was prepared to give. I knew what he meant. I knew that you were the sort of woman who wouldn't be happy with less than true love.

'Tiffany was the self-contained independent type, demanding nothing except the occasional night in bed. We suited each other, understood each other. Both of us went out with other men and women in the course of our careers, but we didn't sleep with any of them. It was the Press who made out that I did. As I said before, Clare, I'm not into casual sex either.'

'And has this Tiffany been home since you met me?'

'She was home when I came back that first Sunday from Bangaratta.'

'You slept with her?' Clare cried, her chest tightening.

Matt shook his head. 'No. We didn't even talk. She was tired and went straight to bed. I meant to tell her about you the next day, but I had an early call and she slept in. By the time I got back a couple of days later, she'd left again to go overseas. New York, her note said. But with no phone number attached.'

Clare turned slowly in his arms to face him. 'And is that where she still is? Overseas?'

'Yes. She won't be back till Christmas.'

'How convenient for you.'

'Oh, Clare...don't be like that. Try to understand. I couldn't contact Tiffany without a phone number.'

'You didn't try very hard, Matt. I'm sure you know the firm she works for. You could have contacted them, found out where she was, found out a telephone number.'

'I suppose so. I just didn't think of it.'

'You didn't want to do it, Matt. You wanted to keep her on tap in case I didn't work out.'

'That's not true.'

Clare did not believe him. Not a word of it. He was another David. A lying, deceiving, rotten bastard whose conscience stopped short of his waist! 'Does this poor woman love you?' she flung at him.

'No.'

'So she just fulfilled your sexual needs,' Clare said icily. 'A job I've acquired while she's away.'

The blue eyes sharpened at her uncompromising tone. 'Now that's enough!' he snapped, his hands clenching into balls at his side. 'I've told you the truth. I love you, woman! I've never proclaimed to be a saint, but I am being honest with you.'

'About as honest as the man who just walked out of here a while ago!' she derided, her face contorted with anger. 'The one you had the hide to condemn when you're no better yourself. You must think I'm a fool,

Matt Sheffield. You wanted your cake and wanted to eat it too. You wouldn't have contacted me again at all if your live-in girlfriend hadn't left you in the lurch. I might give good old Clare another go, you thought. She's a real goer once she's turned on.

'But I turned out to be a bit harder than that, didn't I? You really needed to use all your acting skill. Play the gentleman for a while, send her flowers, ring her every night, make her pant for a while. Then there was the cosy romantic weekend in the country. My God, you must have been furious when it looked as if you'd blown that! But dear sweet gullible Clare still came across after some clever sulking on your part. You must have laughed yourself silly afterwards.'

The blue eyes narrowed and a muscle twitched along his tightly clenched jaw. 'You know that what you're saying isn't true. Seeing McAuliffe again has warped your mind.'

Her laughter made him flinch. 'Oh, of course. And now the reverse psychology bit. Well, answer this, my clever man. Why didn't you tell me yourself about Tiffany, if you loved me so much? Why didn't you tell me you *loved* me, period? You had plenty of opportunity this weekend. Aside from all that, why didn't you have the decency to take me somewhere else? My God!' she spat at him. 'You even screwed me in the same bed, didn't you?'

'I did not! I always went to *her* bed. Always.'

'I don't believe you.'

'I know,' he said, and his eyes hardened.

They kept staring at each other, neither willing to give an inch. Finally, Clare made a move towards the door.

'Where are you going?' Matt demanded.

She stopped and thought for a moment, then raised wretched eyes. 'I'm going to the airport,' she muttered. 'I'll sleep there the night.'

'You're being a fool!'

'No, Matt, I've *been* a fool.'

'What can I say to make this right, Clare? Tell me and I'll say it. I love you, dammit.'

'Do you?'

'Yes!'

'Tough! You had your chance, Matt, and you muffed it. You should have been honest with me from the moment you decided to come after me. You should have told me all about yourself, about your really being a doctor, about Tiffany, about everything. But you didn't. You played games with my life in much the same way you've been playing games with your own.'

'I won't let you go.'

'You don't have any choice.'

'I'll come after you.'

Something deep inside her thrilled to his impassioned vow, but she shook her head, knowing that this was the end.

'I don't like your chances, Matt.'

'We'll see, Clare. We'll see.'

CHAPTER ELEVEN

HOW Clare made it through the next week, she would never know. Matt didn't call. Nor did he come after her, as he'd said he would. By the time the following Saturday morning came to an end and she could hand over the shop to Mr Watson, her depression was so bad that she knew she couldn't face the long afternoon on her own. She needed people around her to stop her from tipping over into despair. Several times that morning she had looked at the bottles of sleeping tablets on the shelves, telling herself that it would be so easy to do what Tilly had done...so very easy...

Sensing that it would be best if she wasn't alone, Clare had a quick bite to eat then set out for her parents' place, certainly a desperation move since she knew her father wouldn't be there on a Saturday afternoon. She clung to the thought that her mother's sarcasm might snap her out of the doldrums and revive her fighting spirit. With a bit of luck Sam would be there as well. No way could she break down in front of her kid sister.

But as she turned into the driveway Clare noticed that Sam's horse, Casper, was missing. Her heart fell, her reaction showing how much she had been depending on Sam being a buffer between herself and her mother.

Agnes answered the door. 'Clare! Whatever are you doing here?'

'Sam's horse isn't in the paddock,' she said tensely. 'Isn't she home?'

'She and Lisa have gone riding together. Did you want her for some special reason?'

'No,' she said in a flat voice. 'I suppose not.'

Clare made no attempt to step inside and her mother began frowning at her. Suddenly she wanted to leave, to run away. She knew Bangaratta had been gossiping about her and her secret city lover—her mother included, from what Sam had told her.

'It can wait,' she said distractedly, and went to turn away. 'I…I'll see you tomorrow.'

Her mother grabbed her arm. 'Clare! Whatever's wrong, dear? Tell me.'

Clare looked back, expecting to see morbidly curious, even ghoulish eyes. Yet all she saw was a very real anxiety…and love…

'Oh, Mum!' she cried and threw herself, weeping, into her mother's arms.

It was some time later before she could speak. To discover an unexpectedly sympathetic mother was both astounding and moving. Clare was not sure if she was crying for her lost love or this newly found one. Her mother really really loved her, she realised in awe. It was heart-wrenching.

'Oh, Mum,' she whispered raggedly for perhaps the third or fourth time.

'Come inside and sit down,' Agnes insisted, 'and I'll make you a cup of tea.'

Clare was led to the kitchen table and forcibly plonked down. The cup of tea took just enough time for her to compose herself.

'I've been such a fool,' she confessed as soon as her mother joined her.

'Things didn't work out between you and your man-friend?'

Clare shook her head, tears welling up again.

'What a shame,' Agnes said. 'It wasn't that David person you used to write to us about, was it?'

Clare had never admitted to her parents that she had lived with David, but since she'd believed she would marry the man she had mentioned him to them in her letters.

'No,' she choked out.

'It...er...wouldn't have been Matt Sheffield, would it?'

Clare's eyes snapped up, her expression giving herself away.

'I thought as much,' her mother said.

'But...but how did you know?'

'I didn't *know*, Clare. It was a guess. Your father muttered something about Matt one night while we were watching *Bush Doctor* and it occurred to me that he might know something I didn't know. You always did confide in your father, never me.'

Clare stared at her mother, whose eyes were revealing a vulnerability she had never seen before. 'It used to hurt me, you know, Clare,' Agnes went on, 'that you always turned to him. Even when you were a little girl...you pushed me away.'

'I...I didn't mean to...'

Agnes sighed. 'No, I suppose not. I dare say it was as much my fault as yours. You and I are as different as chalk and cheese, aren't we?'

'Maybe it's more a case of being too much alike,' Clare ventured, her heart leaping at the obvious pleasure this idea gave her mother.

'Do you think so, Clare?' she said quite eagerly. 'I always thought you took after your father. You're so bright and I'm so…so…'

'Bright,' Clare said firmly.

Agnes looked both taken aback yet thrilled, her reaction tugging at Clare's conscience, bringing forth a shame at the way she had treated her mother. It took two to tango and she had been equally responsible for the deterioration in their relationship over the years. If Agnes had made her feel unloved then it was clear she had also done the same to her mother.

'Mum,' she began tentatively, 'you know I love you dearly…'

'Do you, Clare?' the other woman choked out, her eyes glistening.

Clare stood up and came round to give her mother a hug. 'Of course I do… You've been a wonderful mother.' She sank down in the chair adjacent.

'I always thought you despised me,' Agnes murmured. 'And I guess…I guess I was jealous of you.'

'In what way?'

'You were always so clever…so sure of what you wanted to do. Perhaps that's why I've tried to run things out here. At least I have organising ability, and I wanted to make you and your father proud of me.'

'Oh, Mum! I am proud of you. And so is Dad. He loves you very much.'

Agnes shook her head. 'No…I'm not so sure he does.'

'Of course he does!'

Agnes's grey eyes clouded with distress. 'I wasn't his first choice, you know. There was some girl, in the city. Before he came out here. I got him on the rebound… Oh, Clare! Can't you see? Why do you think he puts up with me the way he does? Because he doesn't care. I keep hoping that one day he'll slap me down, tell me to shut up. Anything to let me know I affect him one way or the other.'

She burst into tears and this time, it was Clare who did the comforting. 'He does love you, Mum,' she insisted. 'He loves you and needs you. And don't you ever believe otherwise.'

'He never says he does,' she muttered miserably.

'I'll get you a drink. We both need something stronger than tea.' Clare jumped up and went over to get a bottle of Muscat out of the cupboard.

'This is terrible,' her mother said when she returned with two full glasses. 'You were the one who was upset and here I am, crying on your shoulder.'

'Don't be silly, Mum. It's so good to be able to talk to you like this. I need a friend just now, and who better than one's mother?'

'Would you like to tell me all about it, love?' she asked, warm concern in her voice.

Clare still hesitated, despite what she'd just said. It was hard to break old habits.

'You don't have to,' Agnes said softly, 'but maybe I could help. I'm not such a silly old fool, you know. One doesn't get to be forty-nine without learning a thing or two about life, and I hate seeing you this unhappy.'

'Yes, I...I'd like to.'

Later, Clare was still surprised by her mother's understanding. There were no gasps of shock, no recriminations. She simply seemed pleased to be in her daughter's confidence.

Clare held nothing back. She even told her mother all about David, so that she could fully appreciate how devastating Matt's treachery had been. What Clare didn't agree with, however, was her mother's view of the situation.

'Poor Matt,' Agnes murmured after Clare had finished.

'Poor *Matt*!' she repeated, astonished.

'Yes...I'm sure there must have been a very good reason why he gave up being a doctor and turned to acting. Maybe he went through some trauma. Maybe a patient of his died or something. And he is a very good actor, dear. Give credit where credit is due. Of course he should have told you about the Tiffany woman, but I suppose he was afraid to. You didn't exactly instil him with confidence in your love, did you? Right from the word go you said you expected the worst of him.'

'And I was right. He's just another David!'

'Is he?' her mother asked gently.

'Yes!'

Agnes sighed. 'What a pity we can't plug people into lie detectors then ask away without their knowing. It would solve so many problems.'

'I think I'm going to get drunk,' Clare pronounced, making short work of her Muscat.

'I'll join you.'

Clare stared at her mother in shock. Simultaneously, they grinned at each other. 'You get the bottle,' Agnes suggested firmly. 'I'll get some bigger glasses.'

Clare was forced to stay the night, being unfit to drive back to town, and the next day she had the most frightful hangover. Serve myself right, she grumbled as she dragged her aching head out from under the pillow. Two pain-killers and three cups of coffee later she was marginally improved. The headache was dulled, but nothing could dull the pain of her broken heart, plus her broken faith.

Matt's not telling her about his being a doctor was not the issue so much as the Tiffany business. Though, when combined, both deceptions spelt a character who didn't really want a deep relationship with her, only a superficial sexual one.

Again and again she went over all the occasions when Matt could have told her about Tiffany. Clare could perhaps excuse his not mentioning the woman at the beginning of their relationship, though she recalled he had asked *her* if there were any other men in her life. But what of later, during the weekend at Three Hills for instance? Or when he'd first taken her to the unit at Kirribilli? No, no, she realised bitterly. Not *then*, not *there*, in *her* place! Clare acknowledged that by then Matt had left it far too late.

Somewhere in the back of her mind a voice kept telling her that it would have always been the wrong place and the wrong time; that Matt could never have won; that she was, as he'd accused, warped by David's actions.

But then cold common sense took over. Stop making excuses for the man, she reprimanded herself. You know damned well he wanted everything and gave nothing. You challenged his ego by refusing to let him make love to you on that Sunday and he pulled out all stops to get you into his bed and keep you there, even going so far as to say he loved you.

'Perhaps you should ring him, Clare,' her mother had suggested the night before. 'Give him a chance to explain further. It seems to me that you weren't too willing to listen to the man.'

Clare had shrunk from the very idea. 'No way!'

'Why?'

'Because he'd just invent more lies.'

'Matt didn't seem like a liar to me.'

'That's what I believed about David once,' Clare stated bitterly.

'But we're not talking about David,' her mother said ruefully.

'Please, Mum...try to understand. I can't ring him,' she had cried. 'I can't and I won't!'

And she didn't.

But her mother's words went round and round in her head, telling her what she knew down deep in her heart to be true. She hadn't really given Matt much of a chance. She'd been prejudiced against him from the beginning, quick to judge and quick to condemn. She'd made him suffer, but more for David's sins than his own.

Clare also kept recalling what Sally had said about people not being perfect, and that if she waited for perfection she would end up a lonely old woman.

Perfection, she conceded, was not only unattainable, it wasn't even desirable. Would she want to live with a perfect man? Good lord, no! He would make her feel totally inferior and inadequate.

All logic aside, however, the overriding truth was that she loved Matt, loved him so much that to contemplate life without him was unbearable. She wanted him back, in her life and in her bed. But would he still want her? Could he forgive her for what she had done?

Clearly, he'd thought about things after she'd left him and decided not to keep hitting his head against her brick wall.

Oh, Matt...

By the following Wednesday evening Clare summoned up the courage to do what her mother had suggested. Call him.

But where? He never had left her a number.

First she looked up Bill Marshall in the Sydney telephone book. It was lucky he'd put 'agent' behind his name because there were hundreds of W and B Marshalls listed. He answered on her third try, the other two times getting an engaged signal. No doubt he did a lot of business on the phone.

'Sorry, Clare,' he told her when she asked how she could locate Matt. 'I have no idea where he is. Shooting finished for the year last week and he just took off for destination unknown. He does that every time he gets some time off and he never says where he's going. I wish I could help you. Look, why don't you try his mother? She might know where he is. Even if she doesn't, he's sure to come home for Christmas which is only two weeks away. I'll give you her number.'

Ringing Matt's mother was a lot more nerve-racking than ringing Bill. Clare hadn't forgotten the woman's attitude towards her, a combination of coldness and snobbish reproof.

'Helen Sheffield,' she answered in her cut-glass voice.

Clare's heart was pounding. Dear heaven, what an intimidating woman!

'It's…er…Clare Pride here, Mrs Sheffield,' she began shakily. 'You probably don't remember my name, but…'

'Oh, but I do remember you, dear,' she broke in, astonishing Clare with her instant warmth. 'I'm so glad you rang. I've been feeling awfully guilty about the way I treated you the night we met. Do you forgive me for being so rude? My only excuse was that I was terribly upset, as I hope you can imagine…and understand…'

'Why, yes, of course I understand,' Clare returned, flustered by this about-face. 'How is…er…Tilly, by the way?'

'Much better. She's finally realising how lucky she is to be alive, and *not* about to be married to that dreadful man.'

'I'm glad to hear that. Er…Mrs Sheffield, I have a favour to ask of you.'

'Yes?' A wariness now, in her voice.

'I'm afraid Matt and I have had an unfortunate tiff—which was all my fault—and I want to contact him but he seems to have disappeared. His agent, Mr Marshall, doesn't know where he is but he said to ring you in the hope that Matt might have kept you informed of his whereabouts.'

'Oh, dear me, no. Matt rarely tells us where he is. He's a most independent man. Of course I am expecting him home for Christmas and he never lets me down when it comes to any important family gatherings, but other than that, I'm sorry, dear. I can't help you.'

'Oh…' Clare's sigh was full of dismay.

'If I hear from him, I'll tell him to call you. Failing that, when he comes home for Christmas, I'll refuse to feed him till he's on the line to you.'

Clare's laugh was wry. 'You're very kind.'

'I'm merely trying to salvage what I'm sure must have been a very poor impression on first meeting.'

Clare wasn't about to deny that this was the case. 'Thank you for everything, Mrs Sheffield,' she said.

'My pleasure, dear. I hope we'll be seeing you again some time.'

'Oh…er…I hope so too…'

But when Clare hung up the phone her heart had never felt so heavy. Somehow, her not being able to contact Matt seemed to be a sign. This wasn't meant to be. She and Matt weren't meant to be.

She threw herself down on to her bed and cried.

CHAPTER TWELVE

THE days dragged. Long empty days, long hot days, every evening spent alone.

No calls came. No letters arrived, not even a Christmas card. Clare watched television every night or read books, but every now and then the print would blur and she would have to put the book down in search of a tissue.

It was a week before Christmas and a Wednesday. Clare opened the shop a few minutes early, a chirpy Sally already there, waiting for her.

'You're going to have to hire a new girl by the end of January, boss,' were her opening words. 'I'm going to finish up then.'

Clare groaned her disappointment. She knew she wouldn't have much trouble filling the position, since jobs were as scarce as hen's teeth around Bangaratta. But she would miss Sally, who was a cheerful soul, with not a bitchy bone in her body. 'Do you really have to finish?' she asked soulfully.

'Afraid so. I want to redecorate around the farmhouse before I get too big to do it. Don't worry, I'll find a good girl to replace me. What about Betty Brown, Mrs Brown's granddaughter?'

Clare grimaced.

'Well, what about...?'

Sally and Clare tossed various names back and forth all morning, till Sally threw her hands up in exasperated frustration. 'I give up! There's no pleasing you, Clare Pride. You've found fault with every person I've suggested. I told you once before: no one's perfect. You have to learn to live and let live.'

Clare looked and felt stricken. She had spent all week remonstrating herself for being inflexible and narrow-minded over Matt, and she'd vowed never to be like that again. Yet here was Sally, showing her that her character's shortcomings were still very much alive and well.

She was deep in depressing thought when the shop's silence was broken by Flora bustling in.

'I knew something would come of having Dr Adrian Archer as guest-of-honour for our ball!' she burst forth, almost beside herself with excitement. 'We have our doctor! Bangaratta has a doctor!'

Clare froze on the spot. Surely Flora didn't mean…? Oh, it couldn't be true!

But what if it was? What if his mother had told him about her call and he'd come rushing out here, prepared to make the supreme sacrifice to win her back?

But she didn't want Matt to do that! He'd said he wouldn't be happy living out here, and just this morning, quite frankly, she'd come to the same conclusion herself. She'd begun thinking about moving back to Sydney to live.

'Who is this doctor?' she asked shakily. 'What's his name?'

'Dr Nigel Ramsbottom.'

Perversely, Clare was consumed with disappointment.

'Get on with it, Flora,' Sally said impatiently. 'Give us some more gen on this Dr Ramsbottom.'

'Well, he's recently arrived from England and is a friend of Dr Archer's. Oh, I mean Mr Sheffield. I can't seem to get it into my head that that's his real name. Anyway, Dr Ramsbottom's in his late thirties and is married with two little children, a boy and a girl. He was looking for a country practice in a small town. Mr Sheffield told him all about us and he's bringing him out today to have a first-hand look. But I was speaking to Dr Ramsbottom on the telephone myself last night and he told me that if we like him, he's ours! Isn't that wonderful?'

'Did…did you say that *Matt's* bringing him out here? *Today*?'

Both Sally and Flora stared at Clare.

Clare gulped. She'd just given herself away good and proper. No one in Bangaratta used a person's first name like that on a short acquaintance. Sitting next to him for just one evening at a ball did not make for a close friendship. Unless of course…

For the first time in years, Clare blushed. Really blushed. She watched, appalled, while all the pieces in the puzzle of her recent behaviour fell into place in Sally's quick brain.

'Clare Pride, don't tell me the man who's been calling you and sending you flowers is Matt Sheffield!'

Clare could feel herself going redder by the moment.

'And you broke it off with him?' Sally squawked. 'Are you crazy or something?'

'Does your mother know about this?' was Flora's first question.

'Of course she does,' Clare said indignantly. 'She's my mother!'

Flora looked flustered at this declaration of closeness. 'But…but…'

'Now look,' Clare said firmly, gathering herself. 'I'm

sick and tired of the way the people around Bangaratta think everyone else's business is their own. So Matt and I went out a few times. So what? Let's not make it into the romance of the century.'

'But it *was* the romance of the century,' a male voice said in a cool calm clear voice. 'It still *is* the romance of the century.'

Clare's mouth dropped open as Matt walked into the shop carrying the biggest armful of roses she had ever seen. Not just red ones. There were white and yellow and pink and champagne as well. He came forward, looking incredibly handsome and rather formal in a pale grey lounge suit, a white silk shirt and subdued grey tie completing the picture of sartorial elegance.

Clare's mouth dropped further open when she saw a crowd of locals following him in, as if he were the Pied Piper. 'Gather round, folks,' he told their eager faces. 'I want you to bear witness for me. I want you to hear what I have to say because Clare has a tendency to doubt my word. But I would not lie in front of the people of Bangaratta. They'd have my guts for garters if I did!'

If Clare had been red before, she was white now, all the blood draining from her face.

'Come out here where everyone can see and hear this properly, Clare,' he ordered.

Before she could respond from her numbed state, Sally took a firm hold of her and propelled her into the middle of the floor of the shop. Matt presented her stunned self with the flowers then proceeded to drop down on one knee in front of her, having produced a small velvet box from his jacket box. When he flicked it open everyone craned forward, the women gasping.

For never had an engagement ring like this been seen around Bangaratta. The diamond was *huge*!

'Clare Pride,' Matt announced in that beautifully modulated voice that made Dr Adrian Archer such a warm credible character. 'You are the only woman I have ever loved. You are the only woman I will ever love. I am asking you to marry me.'

There was dead silence for a few seconds, everyone staring at her with an electric expectation on their faces. Clare felt helplessly caught up in the situation, swept along on a tide of emotion which sent a huge lump to her throat. Her Matt still loved her and still wanted her. Not only that, he wanted to *marry* her!

'Don't make me suffer, woman,' he demanded in a decidedly strangled tone. 'Give me your answer quickly. Yes or no!'

'Oh, yes,' she choked out, her eyes misting. 'Yes, yes, yes!'

Everyone whooped and cheered and clapped, with shouts of, 'Kiss her,' and, 'Put the ring on,' echoing around the shop.

Sally took the flowers out of Clare's suddenly frozen arms, and Matt rose, his own face strained as he slid the ring on her finger. When he took her into his arms, Clare was shocked to feel him trembling. Matt Sheffield, sometime doctor and full-time actor, had just given his most difficult performance.

'Damn and blast, I missed it!' A strange man suddenly burst through the throng.

Clare drew back from Matt's embrace to stare at him, but it didn't take much of a guess to realise that this distinguished-looking but rather pale gentleman with the English accent was none other than Dr Nigel

Ramsbottom. 'Got talking to a chap down the road and lost track of time. I presume all went well, Matt?' he asked heartily.

Matt smiled, nodded and pulled Clare tightly to his side. She suspected that he was finding it as hard to speak as she was at that moment. Her blurred eyes found Matt's again and he bent to kiss her softly on the lips.

'And this must be Clare,' Dr Ramsbottom interrupted, taking Clare's hand in both of his and pumping it. 'I've been hearing a lot about you, young lady. Been giving poor Matt here a rough time. But all's well that ends well, eh what? And don't forget to ask her about that other little matter, Matt. Now! Which one of these other lovely ladies is Flora?'

Clare had to smile as Flora gushed forth. You'll go a long way here, Nigel, she thought wryly. A long, long way...

'What other little matter was he referring to?' she whispered in Matt's ear.

'Perhaps if we could go somewhere private...'

Clare's eyes sought Sally's and Sally nodded intuitively.

'Right, everybody out, please,' she ordered. 'This is a chemist's shop, not Grand Central Station. The show's over, folks. Out, out, out!'

'I won't be long, Sally,' Clare whispered.

'No hurry, boss. Take your time. If any scripts come in that I can't do, I'll improvise.'

'You're a treasure, Sally. Whatever am I going to do without you?'

Sally rolled her eyes at Matt. 'I'm sure Dr Archer will think of something!'

'Sally's leaving your employ?' Matt asked as they walked arm-in-arm upstairs.

'Yes, she's pregnant. I have no idea who I'm going to get to replace her.'

'Maybe no one,' he said cryptically.

'No one?' Clare repeated, closing the door behind them.

'Nigel has a brother who's a qualified pharmacist. He's interested in migrating and buying your business. That's what he wanted me to talk to you about.'

Clare's heart leapt.

'After we're married, I'd like you to live with me in Sydney, Clare. I think that's where we'd both be happiest.'

She smiled. 'I think so too.'

The strain on Matt's face was immediately replaced by a wide grin. 'I was worried I was wrong about that. I thought you'd argue with me.'

'Would I do such a thing?'

'Yes, you spike-tongued witch.' He drew her into his arms and kissed her soundly. 'God, Clare, I was so terrified you'd turn me down. I thought I'd lost you that night… I thought…'

'Hush!' Clare placed her fingers over his lips. 'You're never going to lose me, Matt Sheffield. Never.'

He took her fingers away and kissed them. 'When my mother told me about your call I began to hope, but I wasn't at all confident. I would have understood if you had turned me down just now. It was very wrong of me not to tell you about Tiffany…'

'It was wrong of me to prejudge you, especially over your being an actor.'

'I'm not really an actor, Clare,' he confessed on a

sigh. 'I'm a doctor who played at being an actor for a while.'

'But you're a very good actor!'

'I'm a better doctor.'

'Matt, I wouldn't want to force you into doing anything you didn't want to do.'

'I appreciate your saying that, Clare. I really do. But Dr Adrian Archer will shortly be making his last appearance. I'm going back to being what I always wanted to be.'

'But if you always wanted to be a doctor, Matt, why did you stop?'

'Now that's a long story, Clare. Have you got the time?'

'All my life, my darling. All my life...'

'In that case it can wait till after I do this some more.' And he bent to kiss her again.

It was some time later that they got round to talking, Matt stretched out on the divan with his head resting in Clare's lap.

'I wanted to be a doctor from the time I was twelve,' he began while Clare stroked his hair back from his forehead. 'That was the year my best friend died of leukaemia. He was only twelve too.'

Clare's heart squeezed tight at the note in Matt's voice. He was trying so hard to sound matter-of-fact, but it still hurt, after all these years. She decided not to say a word, fearing Matt might be treading some fine line by telling her all this.

'He was a great kid,' he murmured. 'A great kid.'

Oh, God. Clare could feel a lump gathering in her throat.

'I vowed on his grave that I would be a doctor when

I grew up,' Matt went on huskily. 'Not an ordinary doctor. A specialist. I was going to make sure no more great kids like Tim would die if I could help it. I went to London to do my training, staying on there after I qualified in one of the best children's hospital in the world. Each year we were making further advances, improving the odds, but somehow…for me…it was never enough…

'We were saving eighteen out of every twenty-five kids who came in with leukaemia, but all I could see were the failures, never the successes. In the end, it was the mothers' tears I couldn't stand. They trusted me with their children, those mothers, and I couldn't bear seeing their heartache. I felt I'd personally failed them.'

Now Clare's eyes were flooding. She couldn't help it. Any moment the tears would spill over and run down her face. She gulped over and over but it didn't help much.

'But you did your best!' she protested, her voice choking on a sob. 'You're not God!'

Matt stared up at her then sat bolt upright, twisting round to gather her against him. 'Oh, my darling, I didn't mean to make you cry. No, of course I'm not God. I know that now. But back then, I think I was trying to be, and trying to be was slowly killing me. I was working twenty hours a day, hardly sleeping or eating. One day, a little girl patient of mine died quite unexpectedly. I'd thought she was going into remission and I'd told her mother so. Facing her was the hardest thing I have ever done. Afterwards, I knew I could not go on.'

'So what did you do?' Clare asked.

'I walked away. I quit. I knew if I didn't I'd crack up entirely. Or kill myself.'

'Oh, Matt…'

'I started acting classes as therapy. After a while I joined a small theatre company in London and had some unexpected success. It seemed I had a natural flair for the art.'

'How on earth did you get the lead role in *Bush Doctor* back here in Australia?'

'By sheer accident. I flew home to spend some time with my family a couple of years back. Tilly has a lot of showbiz friends and briefly fancied herself as an actress. She was going along for an audition for this new television show and dared me to come with her and read for the main part. I have to admit I had the advantage, since the role came very naturally to me, especially the emergency operating scene they had me read. The director was blown away by what he said was my "credibility". When I was offered the job, Tilly convinced me not to tell them about my really being a doctor as it might seem as if I had conned them. She also said I needed a good agent and put me in touch with Bill Marshall.'

'Does Bill know you're a doctor?'

'No. He doesn't. Frankly, I was only too glad at the time to put my medical career behind me. When Tilly coerced our family and friends into closing ranks and not telling the media a thing except that I'd studied drama in London, they agreed. Since I hadn't lived in Australia for years, I didn't have any close friends anyway, only some longstanding ones like Barry.'

'Who wouldn't breathe a word,' Clare confirmed. 'Not even when I asked him.'

'He's a good mate. Even so, he suspected I was beginning to have doubts about what I was doing with my life; that underneath, I was thinking about going back to practising medicine full-time.'

Clare frowned. 'Full-time, Matt? That suggests you'd been doing a little part-time.' Another penny dropped. Well, of course he had. Why else would he have a well-equipped doctor's bag in the boot of his car, if he hadn't been practising his profession?

'I've been working in a clinic on one of the Fijian Islands during my holidays.'

'How did that come about?'

He laughed. 'You know, it was remarkably like one of Dr Archer's adventures. I was on holiday and this island kid fell out of a palm tree practically at my feet, breaking an arm in the process. I just went into action without thinking. Afterwards, the warmth and gratitude of his family made me feel more worthwhile than I had in years. When they told me about a small clinic that an elderly doctor ran on a nearby island, I went to see him and offered my services on a very part-time basis.'

'And you've been enjoying doing that?'

'Very much, though of course it's only general practice. I'm not faced with life-and-death decisions every day. Still, by the time I met you I was already thinking about going back to medicine. My visit to Bangaratta brought it even more forcibly to mind. I'd almost made the decision to do just that when we came across that car accident. That rocked me, I can tell you. My brain told me there was nothing I could have done. The man was already dead. But those old hopeless, helpless tapes went off in my mind, and I immediately began to back away once more, from medicine, from commitment, from caring about anybody or anything too much, including you.'

Clare's heart went out to him but she couldn't find the right words to say.

'For years I'd survived on a steady diet of superficial sexual relationships. I decided then and there that the same would suffice for a few more years. But I was deluding myself, of course. I began to realise it during our telephones calls, but it really hit home the moment you arrived at Three Hills. I'd fallen in love for the first time in my life and, try as I might, I could no longer play games with my life. I was going to tell you everything once I got you alone that night, but then I found out about McAuliffe, after which Jill had her accident and all hell broke loose...'

His sigh carried remorse and regret. 'I think you can guess the rest, Clare. Circumstance gave me an excuse to hide my true feelings for you behind a faąde of lust and I did. I hurt you that weekend, my darling, and I'm so sorry.'

'No more than I hurt you in the end, Matt,' she said softly. 'I'm sorry too.'

'No. You were right to do what you did. It made me wake up to myself about a lot of things. From the moment I thought I'd lost you I was forced to reevaluate everything in my life, to see myself for what I had become. A coward, afraid of commitment and confrontation, especially emotional confrontation. Yes, I took a good look in the mirror and I didn't like what I saw. But once I decided to put myself on the line where you were concerned, I felt revitalised, renewed. And now that I know I will always have you by my side, I feel I can do anything!'

'Er...not quite anything, darling. Let's leave the miracles to the good Lord upstairs, shall we?'

Matt laughed and hugged her. 'If I ever get above myself, I know who'll keep my feet firmly on the ground. You tell it like it is, Clare Pride, and I love you for it.'

'In that case, could I have a more tangible demonstration of that love?'

He frowned. 'I...er...haven't exactly come equipped for that.'

Clare reached up to undo his tie. 'Don't worry,' she murmured. 'If you get pregnant, I'll make an honest man out of you...'

Everything was perfect for a wedding. The weather, the setting. Absolutely everything.

Clare opened the doors that led out on to the balcony and stepped into bright sunshine. A long hot summer had browned the grass in the paddocks but, near the house itself, Three Hills looked marvellous. The extensive lawns were lush and green through abundant watering, the garden beds brimming with blossoms. Multicoloured sweet-peas climbed up the walls while bold marigolds stared undaunted up at the clear sky.

Clare's eyes swept round to where the seats were already in place for the ceremony. Rows of them, with a wide strip of red carpet between, running up to a flower-covered dais. Everything had been arranged where the flourishing native trees would supply some shade from the fierce February sun. Getting married among the blue gums and tea-trees was just what Clare wanted. A country setting for a country girl.

A warm smile lit up her grey eyes. It had been typical of Barry and Jill to offer their place as venue for the wedding, for they were generous, genuine people. The church Clare's parents usually attended in Bangaratta was not nearly large enough to accommodate all the guests, and it seemed only fair to meet Matt's family halfway. Especially since Mrs Sheffield had continued to be so warm and welcoming, even when she'd found out Clare was to be her daughter-in-law. Senator Sheffield had been equally accepting of his son's choice of bride.

'Do call me Charles,' he had insisted when they'd gone to Sydney for a pre-wedding party. 'I can't tell you how relieved I am that Matt is finally settling down. I'm also looking forward to having grandchildren,' he added with twinkling blue eyes.

Later that night, Clare had mentioned his father's wish for grandchildren.

Matt had laughed. 'That selfish old bastard! If he thinks he's going to get his hands on my children when he had little enough time for his own, then he's...'

Clare had shut him up with a kiss and one thing had led to another. Again.

She smiled, hugging the knowledge to herself that that was the night she had conceived, their previous risk-taking not having been at the right time in her cycle. She hadn't told Matt as yet, but he was going to be thrilled when she told him—*after* the honeymoon. She wanted him all to herself for a while.

Still smiling, she turned from the balcony and went back into the white and gold bedroom in contemplation of a brisk shower, but before she made the bathroom, there was a knock on the door and Jill peeped her face inside.

'Good, you're awake. Can I come in? I've brought you some coffee.'

'How lovely!'

Jill—also in nightie and dressing-gown—came in with two mugs in her hand. Both women sat down on the large bed to drink.

'Mmm. Marvellous,' Clare murmured. 'Anyone else up?'

'Not that I know of. I just popped my head into the room next door. Your two excited bridesmaids are still out like lights. But there again, they were up half the night, yakking away as if they were long-lost friends rather than having just met.'

'Isn't it strange,' Clare frowned, 'that Tilly and Samantha get on so well… Tilly's ten years older than Sam.'

'Kindred spirits,' Jill observed. 'Both nature- and animal-lovers. But isn't it great to see Tilly happy? Did you notice that she gave Bill Marshall the eye a couple of times yesterday?'

'No!'

'Oh, yes, she did! And he wasn't exactly fending her off, either. Not that I expected you to notice. When you're with Matt, you wouldn't notice if Mick Jagger walked in.'

'Speaking of Matt…'

'Uh-huh,' came the firm interruption. 'Barry has the groom ensconced in the study and Matt left strict orders that he is not going to see you till the ceremony.'

Clare laughed. 'I wasn't going to ask you where Matt was. I simply wanted to say how happy I was that he'd decided to give up acting and go back to being a doctor.'

Jill nodded. 'He did explain why he stopped, didn't he?'

'Yes, and I was so moved, Jill. I…I cried.'

'Acting saved his life, Clare.'

'Yes...yes, I realise that.'

They both fell thoughtfully silent for a few moments.

'So where are you going on your honeymoon?' Jill asked abruptly. 'Or aren't I allowed to know?'

Clare smiled. 'I don't mind you knowing. Just don't tell the Press. First night at the place in the Blue Mountains, then on to Sydney the next morning to fly to Daydream Island for a fortnight.'

'Gosh! How romantic. Where are you going to live when you get back?'

'We've put a deposit on a house not far from Matt's parents'.'

'You didn't mind selling up your business and moving to Sydney?'

'No. I love Sydney. As for work...I can always keep my hand in working as a locum, but we both want a family straight away.' Clare smothered a smile at the thought that the family was already on the way.

Jill sighed. 'You both know exactly what you want, don't you?'

Clare grinned. 'Yes. Each other.'

'I've never seen a man so besotted with a woman, or vice versa. I'll bet there are a few ladies who'd like to scratch your eyes out.'

'Maybe...' Clare's mind flew to Tiffany Makepiece who was at that moment winging her way to New York to marry the man she'd met on a business trip months before. 'That was why she left so abruptly the last time,' Matt had explained to Clare a while back. 'She'd met someone else and had only come back to make sure of her feelings. When she realised our relationship was well and truly dead, she took off again.'

Clare tried to feel glad that Tiffany had not been hurt. Now that she was secure in Matt's love, she could afford to be generous with the woman who'd almost destroyed her happiness.

'Ready, love?'

Clare glanced up at her father then down the improvised aisle at the myriad turned, expectant faces. All her mother's cronies from Bangaratta were there. Even Flora Whitbread. It briefly crossed Clare's mind that her mother would be in seventh heaven for weeks. She only needed one more thing to make her happiness complete.

'Dad...'

'Yes, love?'

'How long is it since you told Mum you loved her?'

'What? Well, I...er...I...why do you ask?'

'You do love her, don't you?'

'Of course! Your mother's a wonderful woman. I'd be lost without her.'

'Then tell her so, Dad. It's important. *Promise* me.'

'I promise, daughter, I promise.'

Clare sighed her satisfaction, her gaze drifting across the aisle to the other side. Matt's parents were smiling at her, but she rather imagined all the other sophisticated guests seated behind them were looking at her and wondering whatever Matt Sheffield saw in a simple country girl.

Clare swallowed.

'Ready, love?' her father repeated.

Her stomach began churning and she turned panicky eyes towards the dais where the four men stood in soldierly formation, grey morning suits giving them a brisk, no-nonsense air. To the extreme right was Mark,

Sam's partner and cousin. Bill was next, groomsman to Tilly's bridesmaid. Then Barry, best man opposite Jill. Finally there was Matt, looking incredibly handsome but frightfully stiff.

As some taped music started to play, his head turned to gaze fixedly at her. Oh, God, Clare agonised. And I said I wasn't nervous!

Suddenly—as though sensing her inner fear—he smiled. It was a smile just for her, a smile full of admiration and reassurance, a smile brimming with hope and optimism, a smile of the deepest love. A sigh reverberted through Clare and tears pricked at her eyes.

'Sweetheart?' her father whispered.

She hesitated, but only for a moment, and only till she had control of the rush of emotion Matt's smile had evoked.

'Ready,' she murmured, then, smiling, took the first step of the rest of her life.